A

Gemma Lawson is a dedicated nurse—
dedicated to the care of others because she
cannot face the pain of her own past. But
in Niall Barratt, head of St Vincent's
trauma unit, she meets a man who has
known tragedy himself, and overcome
it . . .

# A DEDICATED NURSE

BY

JEAN EVANS

**MILLS & BOON LIMITED**
15–16 BROOK'S MEWS
LONDON W1A 1DR

For Katherine

# CHAPTER ONE

GEMMA LAWSON cast an anxious glance at the sky and quickened her steps as the first ominous thunderspots of rain began to darken the pavements. Within seconds it became a downpour and she scuttled breathlessly up the steps and into the warm airiness of Reception, wondering if this was an omen for the rest of the day which had already begun badly when the alarm had failed to go off.

The head porter thrust his head out from behind the hatch and smiled in response to her hurried, 'Morning, Stan,' as she shed the regulation navy coat and searched his desk for the morning's post.

'Morning, Nurse.' Usually a dour little man, he always had time for Nurse Lawson. She was a pretty little thing with those huge brown eyes and a mass of thick chestnut hair which, of necessity, she kept coiled in a neat bun beneath the white cap. 'Today's the day then.' He winked cheerfully and she wished he hadn't because she had been doing her very best to forget. Hence the bad night and the fact that she had only just managed to fall into a heavy sleep at dawn, which was why she had missed the alarm.

She sighed heavily. It was all very well for Sister and everyone else to say she was bound to come through her finals with flying colours. Heaven knows she had studied hard enough for them, throwing herself into it to the exclusion of everything else until even Sister had felt obliged to remark pointedly that, 'All work and no play,

Nurse . . .' But then, Gemma thought, her dark eyes momentarily clouding with the kind of intensity which made them so noticeable and attractive, no one could possibly know just how much it meant to her that she got her SRN.

A smile flicked the corners of her generous mouth upwards. 'I daren't think about it, Stan.'

'Aw, go on, you'll be all right. It'll be champagne all round in the nurses' home tonight. You just see if I'm not right.'

'Coffee more like,' she grimaced. 'I should think it's all any of us could run to.' Her glance went to the clock behind him. 'Oh lor, is that the time? I shall have to make those stairs in twenty seconds flat or I shall be late. And it *would* be Sister Mitford's day on. Is that all the post?'

He handed over the bundle. 'All for now, anyway. I dare say there'll be more when we get the second delivery.'

She wondered, but didn't ask, whether the office had had theirs yet. She and all the rest of the nurses who had sat their finals would be called in soon enough to find out whether the results of the past few years' work had paid off, and suddenly Gemma wasn't at all sure she wanted to know.

'See you later, Stan. I must scoot.' She fled through the swing doors and up the stairs, leaving the head porter to watch and shake his head. There was one nurse he fervently hoped would pass, if only to see some of the colour back in her cheeks again.

Rosemary Ward was in its usual state of uproar of course, and Gemma's arrival was greeted by a sigh of relief from her friend Sue Foster as she bustled down the ward, a giggling child tucked under each arm.

'Boy, am I glad to see you.' She deposited the two pyjama-ed infants into the arms of a nurse. 'Baths for these two I think, Nurse, then breakfast, if you can get them to sit still long enough. Oh, and it's scrambled eggs.' She added the warning, 'Best issue the plastic aprons!'

Jill Crawford beamed, undaunted. 'I'll do my best, Sister. By the way, when you have a minute the senior registrar rang through. He says he'll want the X-rays on young Simon for his round later today so that he can study them before coming to a decision about whether to operate or not.'

Sue groaned as she led the way to the office and gestured Gemma to a chair. 'He'll be lucky. We haven't had them through yet, which means, I suppose, that I'd better get on to X-ray—and they won't like that. They're rushed off their feet as it is. But you know what a stickler our Mr Barratt is. Always expects everything to be done yesterday.'

'Don't they all?' Gemma murmured sympathetically, a slight frown of concentration furrowing her brow as she studied the night report. Her experience of the senior registrar was limited to the visits he made to the ward for his rounds and when, inevitably, she was usually being quietly busy elsewhere, or standing unassumingly in the background as junior nurses were supposed to do.

Oh, she had gained a vague impression, of course, of a tall, austere man in an immaculate suit, whose imperious manner with the staff somehow melted miraculously the moment he talked to his young patients, many of whom were very sick. But as a man? She was unaware that her generous mouth tightened a little. She was probably one of the few who didn't hold any personal views about the good-looking senior registrar and she certainly had no intention of getting caught up in the quite ridiculous wave of romantic speculation surrounding him and every other remotely decent-looking doctor who happened to walk the corridors of St Vincent's. Not that she had ever heard anything specific of course, but then Niall Barratt was a man who liked to keep his private life just that, strictly private. And in any case, senior registrars didn't make a habit of recognising junior nurses as anything more than mere chattels.

Without realising it, her hand strayed in a nervous gesture to push a strand of hair away from her eyes and stayed there to shield a sudden awareness of vulnerability. Oh no, there was no danger that she would ever get involved with any man again. Losing Bill, who had died so tragically and within just a few months of their wedding, was still too much like a raw wound for her to want ever to suffer anything like it again.

Her hand shook, then went purposefully to the report book. No, she wasn't interested in Niall Barratt or any man. Work was the only important thing in her life now and that was the way she preferred to keep it.

Swallowing hard, she tapped the book. 'I see Baby Gregory is down for discharge today.'

'Yes, isn't it marvellous? He's so much better. Mind you, I shall be sorry to see him go. I know you're not supposed to have favourites, but he was gorgeous.'

A smile transformed Gemma's features. 'You say that about all of them!'

'Mm, I know.' Sue stretched and stifled a yawn. 'Gosh, I'm dead.' She grunted and eased off her shoe. 'What you see here is a mere shell. The rest of me lies scattered on Rosemary Ward. If day staff find the pieces perhaps you'd see to it that they get a decent burial.'

'You mean the remains or the unfortunate soul who happens to find them?' Gemma ducked as a copy of the *Nursing Times* sailed past her ear.

'Is this all the sympathy I get? And from my best friend too? I'll have you know those kids have been rushing around since half-past five, and you know it only takes one to set the rest off. Honestly, you wouldn't believe half the little monsters were ill at all.'

She sat up, massaging her toes with grunts of relief. 'Mind you, I must admit I'd sooner see them tearing the ward to pieces than lying in their cots too ill to move.' She winced. 'Sometimes I wonder why I asked for the children's ward at all.'

Gemma got up and went to stand at the glass partition which separated the small office from the rest of the ward. She turned briefly to smile. 'You know jolly well you love it really.'

'Yes, well, just you wait until one of the little demons laces your morning coffee with poster paint. I kid you not, it doesn't come top of my list of favourite flavours. Talking of which,' she consulted her watch, 'I wouldn't mind a cup of any shade or variety right now.'

'Shall I make you one before you dash off?'

'Lord no. I want to get home and get my head down. I'm whacked.' Sue dragged the report book towards her. 'You're covering until Mitford comes on at ten, aren't you? Oh well, you're going to have your hands pretty full until then. I hope she's not late.'

'That's right,' Gemma nodded and felt her heart thud. She hoped Sister wasn't late too, because until she was given permission she wouldn't be able to leave the ward to get her results and it would be awful if she had to hear from someone else who happened to get to the list first, especially if she had failed.

'Don't worry, you'll be all right.' As always, Sue managed to interpret her thoughts and Gemma grimaced.

'I wish I had yours and everyone else's confidence. It's funny—when I finished the papers I felt quite sure I'd done reasonably well, but with every day that's gone by since I've felt less sure.'

'Oh come on! After the way you studied? My dear girl, if they gave medals for sheer determination you'd win hands down.'

Unfortunately, Gemma thought, it wasn't a medal for determination she wanted. Somehow, getting the distinction of the letters SRN after her name was a kind of goal she had set herself as if, in some way, it would be a tribute to Bill, who had shown every promise of being such a brilliant doctor himself. It had seemed natural that, when she most desperately needed something to help her get over that first awful time of grief, she should choose nursing.

She was unaware that Sue was studying her intently and with a faint stirring of angry frustration, seeing the pale features and the faint shadows beneath the thickly fringed eyes. It all seemed such a waste.

'You can't go on like this for ever,' she declared rashly, and saw the faint tightening of her friend's mouth. 'Three years is a long time, you know. For heaven's sake, why not give yourself a chance? I know you loved him, but Bill wasn't the only man in the world you know.'

Gemma stared at her bleakly and wanted to say,

'But he *was* for me,' and knew it would be useless. Stubbornly, she tried to conjure up a mental picture of the man she had planned to marry. It was disconcerting to find that it was hazy, as it so often was these days, and there were even moments when she couldn't quite remember whether his eyes had been grey or blue. She blinked hard, faintly shocked by the admission, and put it down to tiredness. She deliberately changed the subject.

'I see you had an emergency admission during the night.'

Sue Foster resisted the urge to shake her friend firmly and resigned herself instead to going through the report book and the routine of handing over the ward before she could go off duty and to bed in a flat which would be dull and empty because her husband Dick, who was a junior houseman, would have left half an hour before she got home, to go on duty. Sue sighed heavily, knowing that it was the penalty they must pay for her decision to go on working after they had married. Not that there had been much choice really when, like most couples, they needed two wages if they were ever going to raise enough money to buy a house. And they needed the house before they could possibly think of starting a family. It was something she steeled herself not to think about; that, and the rows which seemed to have become an inevitable part of their strained relationship.

She became efficient again. 'Yes, a pyloric stenosis. All the usual signs, projectile vomiting and so on. He went up to theatre and came through the op very well. The mother was told she could stay overnight if she wished, but she has another two-year-old and had to get back so that her husband could go off to work. I expect Sister will have a word with her after visiting this afternoon.'

Gemma nodded, quietly absorbing all the information and trying not to look at the clock. After all, the list wasn't likely to be posted until the DNS, Miss Drake, had seen and studied it first, anyway.

'Look, would you like me to pop down to the office before I go off, and check if there's anything there yet?' Sue hated to see the anxiety in her friend's face. But Gemma shook her head.

'No thanks, there's not much point really, is there?' she laughed wryly. 'I'll go down when I take my coffee-break.' By which time news of the successful applicants would be all over the hospital, she thought dejectedly, and got to her feet as Sue said a weary good night and trundled her way off the ward.

By the time Sister Mitford put in an appearance at ten, all thoughts of the results had been pushed temporarily from Gemma's mind anyway, as the day progressed rapidly from mild disorder to chaos. The fact that it was all perfectly normal for a ward where children were in varying stages of recovery or illness didn't lessen the fact that it was deceptively hard work. Sick children needed reassurance and plenty of love, particularly those due to go for ops, even minor ones like tonsilectomies, and those who were unlikely to recover—as in the case of one six-year-old suffering from leukaemia who was unlikely to survive the next months until his seventh birthday. To Gemma it was the most difficult part of her job, the aspect of it which had, more than once, made her wonder if she could carry on. Yet there was the rewarding side to it too, in the cheerfulness of the children themselves, and incidents like that when another who had been brought in suffering from meningitis only an hour after his sister had died of the very same thing, went home fully recovered. That was the kind of thing which made it all worthwhile.

Sister Mitford sailed down the ward, a stout, large-bosomed figure whose stern appearance fooled only the very newest of probationers since everyone knew that beneath the well-starched apron there beat a heart of gold. Her gaze met Gemma's silent appeal and she shook her head.

'Sorry, Nurse. The list's not up yet. I knew you'd be waiting so I purposely came by the office. Buck up though,' she added briskly. 'You'll be all right It's probably just that the post was late.'

The fact that she knew it wasn't, added to Gemma's feeling of impending doom. It probably meant that the results were so bad that the DNS just hadn't recovered from the shock, or simply hadn't the heart to announce them. But that could hardly apply to everyone, she reminded herself firmly, and hurried across the ward to where Baby Jones was trying to eat his way out of his cot.

'Up you come, my cherub.' She hoisted him up and sat him on her hip as she went in search of a bottle of juice. 'Let's see if we can't find you something a little more appetising, shall we?'

Baby Jones gazed at her adoringly and proceeded to sick up orange juice all over her clean white apron. She was just about to disappear into the office in search of a replacement when Sister beckoned frantically and gestured towards the swing doors.

'Never mind that now, Nurse. Here's Mr Barratt.' Baby Jones was passed to Student Nurse Emmanuel who bore him away, making inexplicable cooing noises which drew a look of resignation from Sister before she tutted briskly at the approaching figure. 'Confound the man. Why can't he come when he's supposed to? He must know he's not due for another hour. Fetch the files will you, Nurse. Quickly, please.'

Sister sped away in the direction of the tall figure who seemed blithely indifferent to the disruption he was causing, not only in Sister's well-ordered life, but in her own too, Gemma thought, sending a resentful glance at the clock on the wall and trying not to mind that this meant she wouldn't get away to coffee and the main office for at least another half-hour.

She emerged from the office and handed the files to Sister before standing as she had been taught, with her hands clasped behind her, telling herself that half an hour wasn't going to make any difference anyway. Whether she passed or not was a matter which common sense told her had been decided the moment she had finished writing the words on her examination paper, and no amount of anxiety on her part was going to change it now. All the same, she felt a vague feeling of resentment stir against Niall Barratt and was unaware that it showed in the look of veiled annoyance she flung in his direction and which made him wonder, not unreasonably, what he had done to deserve it.

'I'm afraid I shall have to do my round now, Sister, if it's not going to cause too much inconvenience. Mr Simkin has been called away unexpectedly and he's asked me to take his clinic.'

'That's quite all right, Doctor.' Sister was already whisking the curtains around young Timothy Barnes' bed in order for the senior registrar to make an examination.

Behind them the general hubbub of noise continued unabated, but if he was aware of it there was no sign of it on Niall Barratt's face, Gemma was surprised to notice. Which was just as well, she thought, because there was no way twenty lively children could be subdued into silence, even for a senior registrar.

She stood quietly as he listened to the chest of a small patient with a history of heart disease, and found herself intrigued by the way in which he seemed able to gain the confidence of even the most fractious child by talking gently and almost making a game of the examination which, though sometimes stressful, was nevertheless vital. She watched the large hands which seemed capable of surprising gentleness and found her gaze straying to the dark hair which curled against the collar of Niall Barratt's shirt. In fact he was quite good-looking in a rugged sort of way, she reflected grudgingly, with the dark hair falling over his eyes and broad shoulders which looked as if they would be more at home in a rugby scrum than in a children's ward, if you liked the type. Which she didn't. The mental note was added defensively. Bill had been more the thin, wiry sort, with sandy-coloured hair . . . Or had it been blond? Her throat tightened spasmodically as she tried to conjure up a picture and it came as something of a shock to discover that the image was decidedly hazy and bore a startling resemblance to the man standing in front of her now.

She blinked hard, realising that the 'image' was in fact reality and that Niall Barratt was staring at her with a look of cool disdain as he said, quietly, 'If you can spare me a moment of your valuable time, Nurse, I said I would like to see this patient's notes.'

She stared down at his extended hand, jumped and slapped a file into it. With the merest nod he opened it and began to read, and Gemma watched Sister's figure advancing hurriedly towards them as she made apologies for having been called away.

'That's quite all right, Sister,' Niall Barratt murmured. Then Gemma caught the slight frown of irritation as it crept into his eyes and he turned to her angrily. 'I asked for Baby Andrews' notes, Nurse, not Anderson.'

Gemma blushed furiously as she found the file thrust into her hands and substituted the correct one beneath Sister's clearly disapproving gaze. 'I . . . I'm sorry, sir, I thought you said Andrews.'

'I assume that you know your patients, Nurse. If so, surely you would *see* the patient I'm referring to.'

His tone was icy and she flinched, knowing that the rebuke was deserved. She hadn't been paying attention, but even as she searched desperately for an explanation, Sister intervened.

'I'm afraid, Doctor, that Nurse Lawson's attention is a little distracted by other things today.' Not, her sharp glance in Gemma's direction seemed to say, that that was any excuse. 'The results of the State Final Examinations come through today and we have great hopes that Nurse Lawson will be among the successful candidates.'

Gemma briefly loved Sister Mitford for her loyalty in implying that, normally, she was a good nurse. There was no answering gleam of understanding in the dark eyes which turned to look coolly into hers, however.

'Examinations may be important, but they aren't everything, Nurse.'

He saw her large brown eyes widen with shock, the sudden stiffening of her shoulders.

'I have to disagree, sir.' She heard her own voice

shaking a little with anger. 'I've worked hard for my SRN. To me it is everything, and I mean to pass.'

The thick brows drew together. 'I would admire your confidence, Nurse, except that I find it a little foolish. Has it even occurred to you that you might fail?'

She felt the sudden wave of nausea in the pit of her stomach and knew that her face was white as the colour drained from it. She wouldn't fail. She mustn't.

For a moment she imagined it was almost pity she saw in his eyes as he watched and interpreted her thoughts. Then she realised it was contempt. 'Be careful, Nurse. Dedication is a fine thing but it can also be dangerous.'

She stared at him, feeling the pulse hammering in her throat, and was glad when Sister's attention was distracted yet again. 'I . . . I don't know what you mean.'

His steady gaze narrowed and suddenly she was aware of a terrible feeling of vulnerability, as if he had broken down her carefully erected barriers and caught a glimpse of what was behind; as if he *knew*. Her breath caught in her throat and she stepped back quickly, suddenly aware of him as a man and some kind of danger, even though she couldn't quite recognise how.

'Don't you?'

She shook her head silently. 'I haven't the least idea what you mean. I fail to see how dedication can be anything but . . .'

'Pure and good and true?' He was laughing at her and she felt the anger rise in her. Then his tone changed abruptly. 'Dedication becomes dangerous when it becomes excessive, Nurse, and when it is misguided. Be careful that you get your priorities right, that you know what it is you really want.' He couldn't help but be aware of her stricken face and his voice softened as he thought, as he so often had in the past when he realised she hadn't been aware of him, that it was a waste to see someone with Gemma Lawson's looks and undoubted capabilities throwing herself and her life away. 'Somehow I don't think you do.'

Her mouth opened and closed and she became faintly aware of Sister returning again to smile at her, apparently totally unaware of anything untoward as she beamed. 'Nurse, I've had a call from Admin.' Gemma felt her heart thud painfully. 'I'm sure Doctor will excuse you just this once.' Her gaze went questioningly in his direction, failing to see the sudden, inexplicable tightening of his lips as he looked at Gemma's white face. 'Well, Nurse,' Sister said. 'Don't just stand there. The results are through. Isn't this what you've been waiting for? Go and find out. Put us all out of our misery.'

Her kindly hand urged Gemma away and with only the merest glance at Niall Barratt's taut face she hurried from the ward, her brain in turmoil. What possible concern was it of the senior registrar what she did with her life? How dare he try to preach to her about what her priorities should be? She knew them perfectly well. She had had plenty of time to work them out. Three years, in fact, and no one, least of all a man with the arrogance of Niall Barratt, was going to make her change her mind.

The doors swung to a close behind her stiff back and Sister Mitford shook her head as she chatted happily to the man beside her. 'These girls. They get themselves into such a state! But we can usually tell which ones are going to make it to the top and I don't think Nurse Lawson need worry. I know we aren't supposed to have our favourites but I must admit I shall be pleased for her if she gets through. She deserves it. She's worked so hard and perhaps it will help to make up for that awful tragedy she suffered some years ago. I imagine you know about that?'

Niall Barratt didn't look up as he continued to make notes in the file he was holding. 'I'm sure your judgment of Nurse Lawson's capabilities is quite sound, Sister. I also hope she finds what she wants.' He added something under his breath and smiled in response to Sister's questioning gaze before he handed her the file and strode out of her ward.

By the time Gemma had made her way down the stairs the inevitable crowd had gathered in the Admin block and she had to fight her way through. The noise was incredible as nurses whose faces she recognised as having gone through PTS with her clamoured to offer congratulations or commiserations and came away either with cries of joy or the look of stunned misery which told the story clearly enough without words.

She saw Anne Hayward, her friend from Men's Medical. The pretty, dark-haired figure saw Gemma and screamed, 'I'm through! I can't believe it!' Then Gemma felt herself spun round, hugged and patted on the back by those who knew at last that all their hard work had paid off and their futures were secure, before she managed to detach herself and walk, numbly, towards the office door.

'Go on in,' Anne urged.

But suddenly Gemma's legs felt like jelly. 'I don't think I dare.'

'Don't be crazy. You'll be all right.'

Even as she walked into the office and faced a smiling Miss Drake, she still found it hard to shake off the feeling that it was all part of a nightmare. Even as she sat with hands neatly folded in her lap and was handed the letter, heard the DNS say, 'Congratulations, Nurse. Well done. Though I must say, it's only what we all expected . . .'

Gemma stared blankly at the details before her. She had passed. She was a State Registered Nurse.

'I'm sure you must be very pleased.'

'Yes, Miss Drake.' She felt cold, clammy.

'I don't suppose you've made any plans,' Miss Drake said. 'Unfortunately I can't automatically offer you your Staff belt, but there is a possibility there will be a vacancy soon, which would mean you will get your promotion. We have someone leaving on Casualty, although nothing is definite yet and I can make no promises.'

Casualty? Perhaps she had misheard. Gemma stared blankly, feeling the wave of disappointment wash over her. It wasn't possible. Of all the wards she had imagined being sent to, the A and E Unit was the one she had never seriously considered. She knew, of course, that some nurses loved it, simply because the patient turn-over was so brief, too brief to allow for any involvement. But that was just what she wanted, to feel some kind of personal commitment.

Protests faltered on her lips, however, as Miss Drake rose to her feet. 'Yes, well I'm sure none of this is really sinking in yet. By tomorrow you'll have adapted and will have had time to become accustomed to the idea.' She smiled, extending her hand. 'Off you go then, Nurse, and perhaps you'd send the next nurse in.'

Gemma walked out of the office. 'I can't believe it.' But Anne Hayward was having no similar trouble.

'Isn't it great? Just think, no more swotting, no more lectures! Well, not until we go for Midder, anyway.' She stopped, flushed with excitement, to ask, 'I say, you are going to do your midwifery, aren't you?'

Gemma laughed. 'I don't know! I can't think straight yet. I have to get used to the idea that I've passed, first.' Her gaze flickered up to the clock. 'Oh lor, I'd better get back to the ward. I'm only here by special dispensation.'

She waved and began to walk along the corridor, surprised to feel a fleeting image of herself in twenty, thirty years time, looking as Miss Drake did now, a slim, attractive, grey-haired figure whose life had been dedicated to the sick, and who, presumably, had no regrets that she had never married, that the hospital had become her life.

She pushed the thought away quickly. Everyone spoke as if it was all over, as if she should be pleased, and she was. But what about the future? How was she going to fill the emptiness now?

She was so engrossed in her thoughts that she didn't see the tall, dark-suited figure until he was standing directly in front of her, making no attempt to stand aside to let her pass.

She looked up, facing Niall Barratt, and wondered why her heart fractionally missed a beat, telling herself that it must still be reaction to the news.

'You made it then.' There was a note of mockery in his tone and she couldn't resist seeing his words as a challenge. There was something about him which seemed to make her want to retaliate. Her chin rose.

'Obviously you doubted it, sir.'

'Not at all.' He seemed only mildly surprised. 'I

never doubted that your kind of dedication would win its just reward in the end.' His mouth twisted in what she thought must be wry amusement. Then, before she knew what was happening, he had bent and his lips brushed lightly against her own. 'Congratulations.' He straightened up and she saw the cool amusement in his eyes. 'Dare I hope that, perhaps now, your work will have your undivided attention, Nurse Lawson?'

Her mouth opened and snapped to a close as she stared after his retreating figure, feeling the colour flame into her cheeks.

'Well really . . .' Mr Niall Barratt needn't have any fears on that score, she thought, turning to make her way in high temper towards the ward. From now on, more than ever before, her mind would be kept strictly on her work, to the exclusion of all else and particularly the senior registrar.

Though why he should be singled out as a special source of danger still hadn't quite occurred to her as she stormed back on to the ward and began to splash orange juice with rather more vengeance than usual into the rows of plastic beakers.

# CHAPTER TWO

THERE WAS a muffled exclamation of protest, a sharp slap on a bare buttock and Sister's voice said briskly, 'There we are, all over. My goodness, what a lot of fuss for one small injection! Right now, back into bed with you and Nurse will tidy you up.'

Sister emerged from behind floral curtains to beam knowingly at Gemma. 'Well done, Nurse. You passed, of course. Yes, well it was a foregone conclusion.'

Curtains were swept back to reveal young Shane Williams' indignant face making vengeful grimaces behind Sister's back. Without turning, she said coolly, 'That will be quite enough of that, young man. It's all for your own good,' before she bustled along the ward, stainless steel dish borne aloft, Gemma at her side. 'You look a little dazed.' She glanced up from the wash-basin where she was scrubbing her hands. 'I suppose it's natural, but it's only now the real work begins, you know.'

Gemma followed her into the office and stood, hands behind her back, as Sister foraged on her desk for some elusive scrap of paper before she sat down.

'Passing your exams is only the start, a goal you must reach before going on.' She studied the pale, silent girl in front of her and smiled gently. 'Don't worry, you'll do nicely. I have great hopes for you, Nurse.'

With an effort, Gemma dragged herself out of a

kind of stupor into which she had fallen. 'I hope you're right, Sister. I'd hate to let you down.'

'Nonsense. You'll be getting your Staff's belt before too long, I dare say.'

'Yes, Miss Drake did mention it but said she couldn't make any definite promise .'

'Unfortunately these things aren't automatic. I only wish they were, but I'm sure you won't have to wait too long.' Her glance flickered over Gemma's neat figure. 'I shall be sorry to lose you.'

Gemma's eyes widened. 'Well in that case, Sister, do I really have to move? I mean, surely it isn't necessary . . .' She was suddenly aware of a look of disapproval. 'That is . . . well I mean, I'd rather hoped I'd be able to stay on here for a while. I like it on the children's ward. They seem to like me.' She broke off lamely as Sister's eyebrows rose.

'*Like* you, Nurse?' Sleeves were rolled down briskly and for the first time Gemma was made uncomfortably aware that she had displeased. 'My dear girl, of course they like you. Children are amazingly adaptable creatures but I fail to see what that has to do with it. This hospital doesn't hand out awards for popularity you know, Nurse. You're here to do a job and to do it wherever it might be deemed most necessary.'

'Yes, Sister,' Gemma felt her cheeks redden. 'I realise that, but . . .'

'I'm sure it would be very nice if we could all do just as we pleased.' The shrewd gaze swept critically over her, then relented a little. 'Unfortunately it isn't like that, as you will soon find out. In fact a move is probably the best thing that can happen to you. It doesn't do to become too comfortable or complacent, too isolated from what is going on around you.'

'Oh, but I haven't, Sister.'

'No?' The stern features for once showed no sign of understanding. 'Well I'm glad to hear it, Nurse. For a moment I thought you were going to disappoint me. Now, do you think we could get on with some work? Perhaps you could make a start on the medicines. Oh, and remind young Jonathon that he goes down to physiotherapy this afternoon, will you?'

'Yes, Sister.' Gemma knew she had been dismissed. She watched the retreating figure, wondering why she had the sudden feeling that she had been reprimanded rather than praised. She shook her head, forcing herself to set about the routine of the ward but not quite able to dismiss it from her mind. What on earth had Sister meant by saying that perhaps it would be a good thing if she were moved, as if to imply that, somehow, she had allowed herself to settle into a nice, protected little rut? It wasn't true. Her cheeks were still flushed with indignation as she bent to pick up a scattered array of comics and plastic bricks. It couldn't be true. Could it?

For the rest of the day it was as if the world conspired to keep her constantly on the move and it was a relief to be told, finally, that she could escape to lunch for an hour.

Needless to say, the cafeteria was crowded. Gemma stood with her tray loaded with a plate of steak and kidney pie and two veg and was just resigning herself to having to eat it standing up when she saw Anne Hayward waving frantically from a seat by the window.

'I was watching for you.' She shifted a pile of dirty cups and plates aside and Gemma disgorged her own crockery into the space before edging herself into the seat with a sigh of relief.

'Thank heavens! Why on earth is it so rushed today?'

'Must be the staff shortages. Everyone covering for everyone else and taking late lunches.' She peered peevishly at Gemma's plate. 'You're not really going to eat that, are you?'

'You bet. I'm starving. I skipped breakfast because I was too nervous to eat.'

'Yes, well so am I. But I've decided the sacrifice has to be made and it's salads for me from now on or I'll never get into a decent-sized new uniform.'

Gemma swallowed a Brussels sprout and with it an odd pang of jealousy.

'You've been made up.'

'Yes, isn't it marvellous!' Anne's eyes gleamed. 'Junior Staff on Women's Surgical. How about you?'

Gemma battled with the quick and very alien feeling of resentment, saying dispiritedly, 'I haven't heard yet. The DNS murmured vaguely about it not being too long. To tell you the truth, I wouldn't even mind staying on Rosemary.'

'For heaven's sake, haven't you had enough after three months?'

'No, not really.' Her appetite had suddenly vanished. 'As a matter of fact, I rather like children.' She stabbed her fork furiously at a potato. 'At least it's a challenge. I just hope when I do get a move it's to something like Men's Medical or a surgical ward where there's plenty going on.'

'Mm, trouble is, there's no guarantee. I suppose I've been lucky.'

Gemma pushed her plate aside and reached for her tea, stirring it crossly. 'I need to be busy. That's what I'm here for, after all. I didn't go through the misery of all that studying and those exams just to play handmaiden to some jumped-up junior house-man.'

'Oh come on, be fair. We both know there's a lot more to it than that. Anyway, why so bitter? It isn't like you.'

Gemma put her cup down, wondering if that was really how it had sounded. 'Oh I don't know. It's just that I had the idea that once the exam results were through everything would be settled, that I'd be able to get on with some real work.'

'Well give it a chance. Anyway, isn't that what we've been doing?'

'Oh, you know what I mean. I just don't think I could bear it if they stuck me on one of the private wards where there's almost nothing to do all day.'

'Someone has to do it. It's all part of what we trained for. In any case,' Anne studied her friend shrewdly, 'you can't go on forever, you know, working at the pace you have.'

'I don't see anything wrong with simply wanting to give my very best to the job.' The reply was defensive, Gemma knew it.

'I'm not saying there is. Only that sooner or later you're going to have to stop using the job as a buffer.'

Gemma opened her mouth on a retaliation, then closed it again firmly. Why was it that suddenly everyone seemed to be misinterpreting her motives? First it was Niall Barratt, then Sister and now her best friend. Why couldn't they just accept that she liked to be kept busy?

She looked at her watch and pushed her chair back. 'I'd better be getting back to the ward or I'll have Sister on the war-path.'

'But you've still got fifteen minutes and you haven't finished your lunch!'

Gemma stared at the plate. 'I'm not really hungry after all. In fact I think I'm still in a state of nerves. I can't take it in even now that we've actually passed.'

Anne got to her feet too. 'I know what you mean. Mind you, I suspect we'll find out soon enough. Come on, let's go up to the cloakroom. We've got time to tidy up and I want to change my tights.' She grimaced at the ladder tracking its way down from her knee. 'Isn't it awful to feel you've suddenly got to start setting an example? And I haven't even got my new uniform yet.'

They edged their way out of the crowded, noise-filled cafeteria and made their way up the stairs, parting company five minutes later having washed, re-applied make-up sparingly, and adjusted their hair beneath their caps.

'I always feel like holding out my finger-nails for Sister to inspect,' Gemma giggled, her temper restored as she pushed open the swing doors. 'I can just imagine the comments. "A nurse's hands are always on display, Nurse. We do not eat our nails. If we are hungry we eat properly balanced, nourishing meals."'

Laughter bubbled over and she turned just in time to catch the slightly disapproving gaze of the man who walked past, reaching out to hold the door before it could close. For some reason her laughter faded and a slight tremor ran through her as she watched Niall Barratt's retreating figure.

She didn't know why she half-hoped he might look back as she watched him through the circle of glass in the doors. The truth was, he probably hadn't even recognised her. She wasn't sure why the thought should leave her feeling vaguely depressed as she waved her goodbyes to Anne and they both fled in opposite directions to make it to the ward with only seconds to spare . . .

# CHAPTER THREE

THERE WAS a frustrating normality about the week
following the results. Gemma's expression,
reflected in the driving mirror of the bright blue
Mini, was tinged with annoyance as she manoeuvred expertly through the traffic towards the
hospital. She gazed with mingling emotions at the
sprawling Victorian building which had gained a
variety of appendages throughout the succeeding
decades. The main block looked shabby and badly
in need of renovation. Something which, she supposed, like everything else these days, became a
matter of priorities. And, after all, it was what went
on inside a hospital which counted, not exterior
appearance.

She turned the corner, heading up the hill for the
car park, passing the ENT block, several admin
buildings and the orthodontic block which had
been put up as a temporary building some years ago
and still continued to function—as it probably
would for several more years yet. It was all a
comfortable hotch-potch of buildings which had
terrified her during her first days when, as a raw
probationer, she had joined the crocodile of other
overawed, wide-eyed students as they crossed from
the Preliminary Training School for the first real
experience of work on a ward.

It was surprising how quickly they had become
blasé about it. She remembered with a smile being
unable to resist the temptation of whisking along
the corridors, giving every appearance of being

terribly efficient and pretending not to see the envious glances of respect on the faces of the latest intake of young hopefuls who were too innocent to recognise junior staff from senior. It had seemed funny at the time. But now, suddenly, the game was over. It was all frighteningly for real. A lot of responsibility went with those letters she had fought so hard to put after her name.

She drove past the building site spread out on a slope running down below the car park. Work had begun a year ago on the new Trauma Unit which was due to be completed in a few weeks' time and would open its doors shortly after for the admission of its first patient. There was a kind of irony in the fact that it should be built now, and especially here at St Vincent's. Too late to help Bill.

She averted her eyes, conscious of her hands gripping the wheel as she swung the Mini into a vacant space, stepped out and locked it.

She was early and paused for a minute to look around. It wasn't often she had the chance, but today, since it was her half-day, she had brought the car, promising herself she would go into town after lunch and do some shopping, not least for a replacement pair of the sensible, flat shoes which were a standard part of the uniform.

There was the first real smell of autumn in the air as she turned and began to walk towards the entrance. The hospital was built on a hill and a faint mist still hung over the fields and part of the town below, giving it a falsely ethereal look which, once it cleared, would fade sharply back into the reality of a busy, productive town. Then the only haze would be that of petrol fumes! It was one of the reasons she had been glad to find a flat on the outskirts, so that on her off-duty periods at least she could get right away, escape to a completely different environment.

The night staff were beginning to come off duty, wearing their usual look of dazed weariness, as she walked on to the ward. Gemma's arrival was greeted by a harassed third-year who announced, as she swept up a vomit bowl and hurried to a distressed youngster's bedside, 'I'm afraid we're behind this morning. This little chap was admitted about half an hour ago and is down for theatre as soon as possible.'

Gemma had already taken in the feverish little face. 'Appendicitis?'

'Mm. His mum thought it was too many apples and fed him a hefty dose of laxative, which hasn't helped matters. Still, we'll soon have you all sorted out, won't we old chap?' She mopped the hot little forehead.

'Has he had his pre-med?'

'No, I was just about to do it.'

'Shall I? You're due off anyway, aren't you?'

'Oh would you? Bless you. I still have to finish the TPRs.'

'Any idea where Sister is?'

'In the office, I think.'

'Right, I'll just do this pre-med, then pop in and take over officially. It's Mitford's day off and I finish at one.'

'Lucky you.' Mary Grover sped away, leaving Gemma to administer the pre-med injection and chat soothingly for a few minutes before making her way to the office.

'Morning.'

Sue Foster was replacing cards in the file and seemed in no great hurry to be sociable as she muttered a response. Gemma perched on the desk, drawing the night report book towards her, mentally noting the details.

'It's still a bit murky out there.' She nodded towards the window. 'Underneath all that mist there probably lurks a fairly decent day. Not that you'll see much of it, of course,' she added sympathetically, then wondered if she had overdone it as something suspiciously like a sob came from the direction of her friend's averted figure. She stood up.

'Sorry, I didn't mean to depress you that much.' Then her smile faded as Sue turned, a large hanky pressed to her nose. 'I say, is something wrong?'

'No,' Sue sniffed. 'Just starting a cold I think. There's a lot of it around.'

'Is there? Funny, I hadn't noticed.' Gemma studied the red eyes and sodden hanky. 'You're not a very good liar. Why don't you tell me about it?'

'Oh damn.' Sue blew her nose hard. 'Sorry about this. It's ridiculous really.'

'Well, far be it from me to pry, but is there anything I can do? How about a cup of coffee to start with?' Gemma moved to flick the switch on the electric kettle.

'Oh no. Honestly, I don't think I could face it. Anyway, I'm all right really. Just being silly.' She sat in the chair and Gemma followed suit on the other side of the desk. 'I ought to be getting on. The ward's in chaos.'

'It will wait for five minutes. Anyway, don't worry. I'll catch up.' Gemma laughed. 'That's one advantage of Mitford being off.' She became serious. 'Do you want to talk about it, whatever it is? You haven't . . . Well, you and Dick haven't had a row or anything like that have you?'

This time there were definitely tears. 'Not a row exactly. Well, not really. Dick has a weekend off soon and you know how rare that is.'

'So what's the problem?'

Sue laughed tearfully and blew her nose. 'We'd sort of planned to go down to Exeter to see his family. It's been ages since we were last down there and now, wouldn't you just know it, I have to work.'

'Oh no. That's rotten luck.' Gemma digested the implications. 'Well, couldn't you ask to change duties with someone else?'

Sue licked her lips wryly. 'I've already tried, but you know how things are at the moment and night staff are even more short than you are on days. Anyway, it's not really fair to off-load on to someone else, is it? We all like weekends off.'

'I would have thought Dick would understand. He's not usually unreasonable.'

Sue didn't meet her gaze. 'I tried to explain. He said he didn't see why it had to be me, that weekend of all weekends. He knows I'm covering because there are no other senior staff available, but he seems to think I'm just being unreasonable.'

'That's not like him.' Gemma frowned unhappily. 'I wish there was something I could do.'

'Oh, that's all right. I expect we'll sort something out. We'll get over it. We always do. I just hate it, though, when we fall out, especially over my job. And Dick goes all silent on me, as if it's my fault and I asked for this duty.'

'I'm sure he doesn't really think that.'

'The trouble is,' Sue Foster's face was drained of colour, 'he really thinks I should give up my job.'

Gemma looked keenly at her friend's unhappy

expression, not sure what to say. 'Do you think he's right?'

'No I don't.'

Gemma subsided. 'I'm not saying I do, either. You know I don't like taking sides, especially where two of my best friends are involved, but you obviously aren't happy as things are and you've said yourself that the only time you get to meet is when you pass on the stairs as you're about to fall into bed and he's on his way out.' She frowned. 'It's different for me. I don't have anyone else to think about.' She could have bitten her tongue out as she saw the sudden painful drawing together of Sue's brows. 'I didn't mean that the way it sounded. I just meant . . .'

'It's all right. I know what you meant, and I do think about Dick all the time. That's the trouble. I hate this arrangement as much as he does, but when we got married we decided—together, it wasn't just a one-sided thing—that before we could even think about a family we had to get some money behind us to buy a house. We talked about it for ages, so it's not as if we went into this without knowing what was involved.' Sue's eyes were bright with unshed tears. 'I hate working nights, but I do want that house. The flat we're in now is awful. It's old and cramped. It hasn't even got a bathroom. So how could I possibly give up my job now?'

Gemma wished she had some answer other than the obvious one. Instead she was simply aware that talking hadn't helped. 'Well, you know Dick, I expect he'll soon get over it.'

'You could be right.' But there was a large note of doubt in Sue's voice. 'He says he's going to see his parents alone, anyway, and that perhaps we'd both better do some serious thinking while he's away.'

'But that's hardly fair,' Gemma retaliated involuntarily.

Sue sighed, wiped her eyes and got to her feet. 'Yes, well perhaps he's right. Perhaps I do need to do some thinking. The trouble is, I'm not sure I can come up with the answer he's looking for. Still, it's hardly your problem. Like I said, I'll sort something out—and right now it had better be my ward so that I can hand over and get off and let you get on with your own work. Otherwise we may both be looking for a new job.' She smiled wryly. Gemma listened to the report, asked several questions, was given the keys and watched her go, wishing she could have done something to relieve the look of tension on her friend's face.

Departing night staff and the clock told her she had better put it from her mind, but she was still left with an unpleasant feeling of helplessness. Sue and Dick Foster were both her friends. She had watched their courting, been at their wedding. She could only hope she wasn't about to witness the break-up of what had seemed an ideal marriage. She shook herself out of a feeling of depression which was threatening to take over and marched briskly on to the ward.

*Men*, she thought crossly, as the swing doors opened and Niall Barratt chose that precise moment to enter the ward. Why did they always have to complicate things? Well, she had no intention of allowing them to do so in her own life. With which thought she advanced to meet the senior registrar, flinging a look of vindictive warning in his direction as she handed him the first file and marched primly towards the first patient.

To her chagrin, however, he stood with the unopened file in his hand, frowning at her as if something in her appearance displeased him. Her hand went automatically to her neat collar. Perhaps a smudge . . . but no, she had checked, as she always did before appearing on the ward, that her appearance was satisfactory. She frowned hesitantly.

'Is something wrong, sir?'

For a moment he continued to stare, then his mouth grew taut and he flicked the file open impatiently. 'Yes, I'd like to get on, Nurse, if you would be good enough to tell Sister I'm ready to do my round.' He looked pointedly at his watch and failed to see the brief look of anger which registered in her eyes before she said, with as much control as she could muster,

'I'm sorry, sir, but today is Sister's day off. I am in charge.' Inwardly she seethed with fury at the implication that he considered her incompetent and her chin rose fiercely. 'I'm sure I am perfectly capable of answering any queries you may have.'

The dark gaze honed in on hers until she almost flinched before the cool scrutiny. 'Ah yes, I'd forgotten. I suppose I should be addressing you as Staff Nurse, shouldn't I?'

She felt her pulse accelerate as she sensed his quiet mockery. 'There's no need for that, sir,' Her voice came out stiff with fury. 'I may be qualified, but my appointment as a staff nurse is by no means automatic, as I'm sure you must be aware.'

Suddenly she thought it couldn't come quickly enough if it meant she would get away from Niall Barratt's overbearing manner. He had no right to treat her like this. More to the point, what had happened to the man who had kissed her? Or was it possible that the incident had, after all, been nothing more than a figment of her imagination? The flush in her cheeks told her that it wasn't so and she was horrified to find his gaze fixed upon her—almost as if he had read her thoughts and found them distinctly annoying.

He flipped the file open again, his tone perceptibly cooler. 'Well, in that case it looks as if I have no choice. I suggest we get on, Nurse. My time is too valuable to waste.'

Clamping her lips upon an obvious rejoinder, she stood aside, maintaining an icy politeness as they progressed with maddening slowness from bed to bed.

'Damn the man,' she thought, when finally the round was over and she had the satisfaction of watching his figure retreat from the ward and could return to the office. She sat at the desk, hands gripped together, staring at the page in front of her but seeing nothing for the sudden blurring of tears which rose, infuriatingly, to fill her eyes.

'Damn you, Niall Barratt,' she muttered, covering her face with a hand that shook. How was it possible that one kiss could affect her so much? Especially when she didn't even like the man and he certainly didn't think much of her, either as a nurse or as a woman.

The thought followed her like a dark cloud as she battled her way through the rest of the morning and finally went off duty and headed for town. But for once the distance between herself and the hospital didn't seem to help. No matter how many miles she put between herself and the senior registrar, somehow or other it seemed he always managed to intrude into her life.

# CHAPTER FOUR

'GARY, WILL you please get off Kevin's chest? I'm sure it can't be doing him any good having you sit on him like that.'

'But I'm giving the kiss of death, Sister.'

Sister's mouth twitched as she caught Gemma's eye and between them they hauled the indignant pair apart. 'The phrase is kiss of life, young man, and if I may say so, the victim looks remarkably healthy to me.'

'But he's not, Sister. He's got an arrow through his heart and another through his head.'

Gemma had to struggle to keep her face straight as the six-year-old filled in the gory details with relish. 'Oh dear, that sounds rather serious, don't you think, Sister?'

'I do indeed, Nurse. In fact, I think in that case he's probably past any help we can give him.'

She bent to hold the limp wrist of the spread-eagled child who groaned, theatrically, 'I'm a goner. You got me, ya dirty rat.'

Sister winced. 'Yes definitely beyond help. There's nothing we can do here, Nurse. Unless . . .' She paused.

'Unless, Sister?'

'Unless we get Mr Barratt to fix him up. He's the only one who could do it.'

'And what's all this then?' A voice, tinged with laughter, set Gemma's heart lurching as she whirled round and caught sight of the man who had obviously been standing watching the lurid scene.

Her voice shook a little. 'I'm afraid we have a very sad case here, sir. Perhaps you'd care to take a look.'

Keeping a straight face he knelt beside her to inspect the body. 'Yes, I can see this is a desperate case, Nurse. He's pretty far gone. How did it happen?'

'An arrow to the heart, sir. Oh, and another to the head.' She couldn't resist the smile which tugged at her lips. It faded as he looked at her and she blushed, waiting for the frown of impatience she had seen on the faces of several doctors as they dismissed childish play in a need to get on. In Niall Barratt's case, however, it didn't come.

Instead he stroked his chin, considered the patient thoughtfully and murmured, 'Mm, pretty good shooting on someone's part. I don't know what we can do about this. Any suggestions, Nurse?'

She fell in with him, pretending to speculate seriously. 'Well, a sticking-plaster might help.'

'Yes, you're right, definitely a sticking-plaster. Better make it a very large one.'

'Is that all?' The child suddenly sat up and took an indignant interest. 'You can't plug a hole that size with sticking-plaster!' He collapsed again, groaning and writhing, and Gemma caught the gleam of laughter in the senior registrar's eyes.

'He's right, Nurse. I think this is definitely a case for . . .'

Her hand fluttered to her heart dramatically. She may be play-acting but it was certainly beating uncomfortably fast beneath her apron. 'You don't mean?'

'That's right, Nurse.' Niall Barratt straightened up. 'I'm afraid it looks like a double dose of ice-cream all round. What do you say, boys?'

'Whoopee!' There was little doubt about what the pair thought as they rushed off down the ward. 'Great, Doc! You can be one of the goodies. Bang, bang, you're dead, Nurse!'

Gemma groaned, closed her eyes and pretended to collapse, only to find herself caught in a pair of strong arms which seemed strangely reluctant to release her. Her eyes flew open to stare into Niall Barratt's face and she straightened up shakily, feeling the colour rush into her cheeks.

'I'm delighted to see you believe in entering into the full spirit of things.' There was a suspicion of laughter in his voice. 'I take it you aren't too badly wounded.'

From the way her legs were shaking she might well have been, Gemma thought, detaching herself furiously from his grasp. 'Not at all, sir,' thank you. It's all part of the job.'

'Ah yes,' his eyes narrowed. 'The job.' He released her abruptly, almost as if he sensed the discomfort she felt at his touch, and she backed away, straightening her apron, realising with a sense of shock that Niall Barratt could do things to her emotions which no one else had in a long time.

'Excuse me, I have to . . . I have to get the tables.' Confusion made her movements jerky as she turned away and began to draw the bright red tables into the centre of the ward and set out jigsaws and an assortment of toys. She hoped he would leave as soon as the round was finished, but he was still there when she emerged from the toy cupboard, her arms full of books, and she couldn't help but be uncomfortably aware of him as he strode up the ward in search of Sister.

The tables organised and her young charges

happily ensconced, Gemma went to one of the cots, letting down the side so that she could lift the tiny occupant out. The baby was three months old and had been admitted with pneumonia, but she was recovering rapidly and regaining her former chubbiness.

Gemma felt her heart jolt as she cradled the infant in her arms, swaying softly as she made the universal baby sounds. Once, an eternity ago, she and Bill had talked about having a family. She tried to imagine them now, laughing, dark-haired children. Her eyes widened in sudden shock. Dark-haired? Now why on earth should she think that? Her gaze rose and went unthinkingly to the far end of the ward, to the figure who was watching her, a faintly quizzical, or was it amused, look on his face.

She turned her back hastily on Niall Barratt and bent to the task of changing the baby's nappy. A few minutes later she was aware of the senior registrar walking up the ward and breathed a sigh of relief—until a voice spoke, softly, far too close to her ear.

'You should spread a little of that dedication around more often, Nurse. It suits you.'

There was an unreadable expression in the eyes which stared down at her and Gemma flushed, hating him for having caught her unawares. And worse, she suspected, for having guessed what had been in her mind just for those few tantalising seconds.

She straightened up, feeling suddenly ridiculously vulnerable as she clutched the baby to her, as if it could provide some sort of barrier between them. There was a strangely intent expression on his face as his gaze flickered over her and she said stiffly, 'I take pride in doing my job well, sir. And now, if you will excuse me, I have a lot to do and you are preventing me from doing it.'

His face remained impassive as he dropped the file he had been carrying on to the bed beside her.

'You're right, Nurse. Thank you for reminding me that I have a great deal to do to. In fact,' he glanced at the ward clock, 'I should have been at a meeting five minutes ago.'

He walked swiftly away, leaving her with the uncomfortable feeling that she was going to have to be more careful in future where Niall Barratt was concerned. He had caught her in a weak moment when her emotions had been temporarily off guard. But it was the fact that he had aroused those emotions in the first place which worried her most of all.

It was a relief to be able to get off duty and back to the flat to soak in the long, hot bath she had been promising herself all day. Lying in the water, however, it wasn't so easy to get rid of the knots of tension which her meeting with Niall Barratt had built up and she was scarcely more relaxed when she finally clambered out and slipped into a clean nightie and housecoat before padding into the kitchen to make herself a warm drink in the hope that it might help her to sleep.

She stirred drinking chocolate lethargically into a mug of milk, watching the colours merge. It wasn't even as if there was any reason why she should let him affect her like this, and yet it seemed to happen—that feeling that the moment he walked into view he presented some kind of threat. Chin cupped in her hand, Gemma stared at nothing in particular and was caught unawares by the memory of a kiss and a face which suddenly set her pulses racing all over again. Furiously she put her cup down and went briskly from room to room, plumping cushions with far more vigour than they warranted, tidying magazines and straightening curtains until she came to a halt, breathing hard.

This is ridiculous, she told herself, blinking against the tears that were suddenly blurring her eyes. She hadn't cried in a long time and she had no intention of starting now. She had her future all neatly mapped out and it didn't include getting involved, especially not with a man like Niall Barratt. All the same, it was humiliating to find that when she finally climbed in between the sheets and put out the light, it was his face which intruded into her thoughts and kept her awake far longer than usual.

Gemma woke feeling cross and unrefreshed by the small amount of sleep she had eventually managed to get and, to make matters worse, had to skip breakfast because she was late. And then she found that most of the traffic in the area had been diverted, because of a burst water main, on to the road she normally took to the hospital. As a result she found herself sitting impatiently in a traffic jam, her fingers tapping on the steering wheel as she willed the lights to change.

'Oh come on. *Come on.*' It seemed to take an eternity and when she finally drove into the car park it was with the certain knowledge that, with luck, she would only just get to the ward on time— and without it she would be late.

As it happened she was lucky. Jack Slater, one of the porters, was just taking a trolley up in the lift and saw her as she rushed breathlessly into reception. He held the doors open, grinning, as he guessed the reason for her harassed look.

'Come on, hop in. You'll just about make it.'

With one frantic look around to make sure no one was looking, Gemma leapt in, sighing with relief. Nurses were supposed to use the stairs.

'Bless you. I couldn't face a set-to with Sister, not today of all days.'

'Overslept, did we?'

'Something like that.' Didn't get much sleep at all would have been more like it, she thought ruefully, thanks to Mr Niall Barratt.

'Your floor I think.' The doors slid open. Gemma offered up a silent prayer that no one would see her and fled, throwing a wave. 'Thanks, you're an angel!'

'Any time.' Jack Slater grinned cheekily and went on his way wishing it was every day he had Nurse Lawson to himself, if only for a few seconds.

By an even greater piece of luck, Sister was still in the office going through the night report so that Gemma was able to slip into the kitchen and start helping with the mixing of feeds for the very young babies before anyone could notice her late arrival.

Maria Van Silk, the blonde-haired third year nurse, grinned in her direction from the refrigerator where she was putting the first batch of bottles. 'I thought you weren't going to make it.'

'Phew, so did I. The traffic was awful. Have I been missed?' Gemma went to scrub her hands thoroughly at the sink. 'Here, let me help with those.'

The Dutch girl shook her head. 'Sister Black is still in the office, so I think you're safe.'

'Oh lor, yes! I forgot it was Mitford's day off. Anyway, I wouldn't count on it. Sometimes I think all sisters have eyes in the back of their heads. Is Baby Watson still on three-hourly feeds?'

'I think so, but he's picking up nicely so perhaps not for much longer.'

They chatted companionably as they worked, the sound of breakfast being served going on in the ward, the telephone jangling, people coming and going. Whatever else you said about Rosemary Ward, Gemma thought, it was never quiet.

'Aren't you off on leave soon?'

Maria smiled. 'I go tomorrow.'

'Lucky you. I've never been to Holland.' Gemma indulged a brief vision of getting away from it all and came back to earth with a sigh. 'I've heard it's beautiful.'

'Yes it is—at least where I come from. You should try it some time.'

'Where exactly? Amsterdam?'

Maria laughed. 'Wc don't all live in the big cities, you know. As a matter of fact I come from a small town. Papendrecht.'

'Papendrecht.' Gemma rolled her tongue round the sound and laughed. 'It sounds marvellous.'

'It is. Why don't you come over some time and stay? My family are always pleased to welcome my friends and we could take you sight-seeing—to Ooblasterdam perhaps, to see the windmills along the canals.'

'You mean they do still really have them?'

'Oh yes. Some of them are very old, many hundreds of years. You can look round them, see how the people used to live.'

'Uncomfortably, I should think. Weren't they a bit cramped?'

'You'd be surprised how much room there is, how cosy a windmill can be. But the winters, I don't think those you would like because the wind is very cold and the land very flat.'

'Quite a change from here I should think,' Gemma murmured, vaguely envying her friend. She bent to the task of scooping milk powder. 'Will you fly?'

'No, I can drive quite easily. I cross on the ferry. It takes two hours maybe to drive to Antwerp and then maybe another hour to my home. With all the luggage I have, all the presents I take,' she smiled, 'the car is best. Maybe next summer you'll come for a holiday. We could go shopping and have coffee and large slices of gateau.'

'Oh don't!' It sounded marvellous and an eternity away. A year ahead was too far to contemplate, something Gemma had taught herself not to do. And in any case, the thought intruded sharply, a lot could happen in that year. It was impossible to know where she would be or what she would be doing, now that St Vincent's had suddenly become too small to hold both herself and the senior registrar.

She was shaken out of her reverie by the summons to Sister's office, where the Kardex was read and each nurse allotted her various duties for the day. Gemma had looked for Sue Foster and felt annoyed with herself for having arrived late and missed her. Oh well, she would just have to wait until tomorrow to find out whether Sue and Dick had been able to resolve things.

As they all filed out of the office, Sister Black called Gemma back. She returned to stand before the desk and the attractive, tall figure with dark hair who looked up and frowned.

'Will you pop down to Casualty as soon as possible, Nurse, and see if you can chase up young David Keene's notes? He was sent up with just the admission details but I gather he has been an in-patient previously and we shall need the case notes. I've spoken to Records, who for some reason best known to themselves sent them to Casualty instead of to us.'

'I'll go straight down now, Sister.'

Paula Black looked up and smiled. 'I haven't congratulated you yet, by the way. I should think the results took a weight off your mind. I remember I went through agonies waiting for mine.'

'I know what you mean,' Gemma smiled shyly. 'It wasn't exactly the kind of experience I'd care to repeat too often.'

'Well, hopefully you won't have to—at least, not yet awhile, unless you decide to go on and get more qualifications. What about midwifery?'

'I haven't really decided.' Gemma felt the slight quiver of guilt. For most other nurses it was all decided, almost a foregone conclusion. 'I don't honestly know what I want to do.'

'No, well it's not important. You don't need to make an immediate decision. In any case, we don't all want to become midwives, which is probably just as well.' Paula Black smiled. 'I should think you'll be made up to Staff fairly soon, anyway.'

'I hope so. I'd like to feel it all meant something, if you know what I mean.'

'You haven't thought of applying for a post elsewhere?'

'No, not seriously.' At least not yet, Gemma thought. 'I'd be sorry to leave Vincent's. Oh, I know we have a reputation for being a bit old-fashioned in some things but in those that really count . . .'

'Yes, I know what you mean,' Sister Black laughed. 'Beneath this ancient, Victorian façade we do our humble best to make progress—but as

with most things, it's a case of making haste slowly.'
Gentle humour made her face even more attractive. 'It's one of the reasons why we like to hang on
to some of our nurses. The dedicated ones are hard
to come by these days.'

Gemma heard herself murmuring something in
response, aware that suddenly the word dedication
seemed to have a less than pleasant ring to it.

'By the way,' Sister said as Gemma headed for
the door, 'the DNS would like to see you later this
morning. You'd better try and fix a definite time.
Perhaps after your coffee-break.'

'Yes, Sister.' She hesitated. 'I . . . I don't suppose you have any idea what it's about?'

Paula Black was already immersed in her work
and scarcely looked up. 'No, none at all, Nurse.
Are you due for some leave? It may be that. In any
case, you'll find out soon enough.' She smiled
'Perhaps you can go down on your way back from
your break. Don't be any longer than you can help.'

'No, Sister.' Gemma left the office, a troubled
frown darkening her face as she tried, without
success, to think of some way in which she might
have offended.

Unless, the thought came with almost heart-
stopping suddenness as she flew down the stairs
towards Casualty, Mr Niall Barratt had made some
complaint against her. Perhaps she had spoken a
little sharply when he had come to the ward demanding to see Sister. But that was hardly a sin,
she thought huffily, and after all, she had been in
the right. Not that that was likely to make the
slightest difference to a man like Niall Barratt.

The swing door responded to her outstretched
hand as she entered Casualty and found herself on
the receiving end of several hopeful glances from

the rows of waiting patients. But they all faded quickly as, smiling apologetically, she sped in search of the clerk.

The mauve-clad figure of Staff Nurse Dixon bustled towards her, pausing to give reassurance to a lady whose recalcitrant child proceeded to wail loudly the moment anyone in uniform appeared.

'No, Mrs Watts, Doctor hasn't forgotten you. He'll be with you as soon as possible. Look, would you like to take your little boy into that empty cubicle over there and I'll send a nurse to you in a moment.' She pulled a wry face as she met Gemma's eye. 'We're going to have trouble with that one, I just know it.'

'Is it anything serious?'

Meryl Dixon grinned. 'The child has a positive passion for sticking beads in places where beads were never intended to go. Last month it was his ear, this time his nose. I dread to think where he might try next. Not that it will take long to sort out, but we're having one of our busy bursts.'

She nodded to a cubicle where the curtains were drawn. 'A road traffic accident. Three injured brought in and at least one of them looks as if he may not make it.' She sighed. 'I hate this side of the job and we still have the relatives to deal with.'

'Sooner you than me.' Gemma smiled sympathetically. 'I don't suppose you know where Sister is, do you?'

'Your guess is as good as mine. Up to her eyes, I should think.'

'Okay, I'll manage. I'm only on the trail of some missing case notes.' She was turning away as the curtains parted and a slim, fair-haired figure stepped out wearing a harassed look above his white coat. She waved discreetly, and to her delight Dick Foster came over.

'Hi.' She wrenched her gaze away from the blood spattering his coat. 'Sorry, I didn't mean to waylay you. Nurses aren't supposed to, are they?'

He grinned, briefly relaxing the lines of tiredness on his good-looking face. 'That's okay. Seeing as it's you, I'll forgive you. To what do we owe this unexpected pleasure, anyway?'

He scribbled something on the case file he held and rested a hand gently on her back as he followed her to the desk. 'We don't often see you down here. Come to see how the other half lives?'

'Not exactly. Not that I can say I envy you, anyway. It's all a bit depressing, isn't it?'

He looked around him as if not really seeing it. 'I suppose after a while we just don't notice it, or we become immune. It's probably the only way to stay sane. Not thinking of joining us, are you?'

Gemma's eyebrows rose fractionally. 'No, thank you. I'm tracking down some missing records.'

'Ah, not my department I'm afraid, although I'd love to help you look, if only I could spare the time. You know how it is.'

She did, grimacing sympathetically at the noise which seemed to be a constant part of the background. She liked Dick Foster. He was nice, good-looking and strictly a one-girl guy, unlike some of the other junior housemen she could name, who chased anything in skirts. Which made it all the more depressing to see the look of weariness and dejection on his face as he handed the case file to the girl behind the desk before turning hesitantly back to Gemma.

'You're quite a stranger these days. It seems ages since you came over for a meal.'

'Yes, I suppose it is.' She laughed easily. 'Getting the flat straight seems to have taken longer than I thought, but now that it is, perhaps you and Sue might come over to me.'

She was a little dismayed to see him frown. 'It sounds like a good idea. Unfortunately there may be problems.' He looked at her directly and brushed a hand wearily through his hair. 'I don't suppose you've seen my wife recently?'

She took a deep breath. 'Well . . . actually, no. But then our paths don't often cross, in spite of the fact that we both work on Rosemary.' She laughed and heard the awkwardness in the sound. 'It's ridiculous, isn't it?'

His mouth tightened. 'Oh, I wouldn't say that. We live in the same flat but I sometimes get the distinct feeling I should make an appointment.'

'Oh, surely that's hardly fair?' Gemma said softly. 'I mean, I don't suppose Sue likes it any better than you do.'

'No?' She caught the momentary flicker of bitterness as he reached for another batch of cards. 'Well I don't see her doing an awful lot to change things.

Gemma bit her lip. 'I'm sorry.' She felt her heart go out to him, but how could she say anything?

'Well, it's hardly your problem is it?' He smiled half-heartedly.

'I hope you manage to sort something out.'

'Oh, I expect we will, one way or another.'

He waved and she watched as he made his way back to the cubicles, feeling for some reason irrationally depressed as she turned and made her own way back to the ward, missing records clutched in her hands. If only people realised just how lucky they were, she thought, sighing so heavily that Sister looked at her intently.

'Are you all right, Nurse?'

'Wh . . . Oh yes, thank you, Sister. I managed to find the notes you wanted.' She put them on the desk and returned to the ward where she spent the next hour determinedly doing her best to put Sue and Dick Foster's problems out of her mind and concentrate on the job in hand. She was so engrossed that it came as a shock to hear Sister telling her to go for coffee.

'And don't forget to go to the office.'

'As if I needed the reminder,' Gemma thought, pausing for a moment to check her appearance before tapping on the door and waiting for the summons to enter. She did so to find Miss Drake engaged in a telephone conversation and indicating with a wave of her hand that she take a seat. Gemma obeyed, automatically straightening her skirts and clasping her hands in her lap as she looked around the room. Seconds later Miss Drake addressed her.

'I'm sorry to keep you waiting, Nurse. Now, where was I?'

'You asked to me to come and see you, Miss Drake.'

'Oh yes, so I did.' The DNS shuffled a pile of papers, smiled and withdrew one. 'I'm sure you'll be delighted to hear that we have a vacancy for a staff nurse coming up shortly, and that we intend offering you the post.'

Gemma felt a tremor of excitement run through her. *Staff Nurse Lawson*. For a moment her breath caught in her throat. If only Bill could have known. He would have been so pleased, so proud. She started, drawing herself up, and she realised Miss Drake was speaking.

'I take it you will be accepting?'

It was more statement than question as the DNS's delicately traced mouth formed a smile. She had been watching Gemma intently, accustomed to the reaction this kind of news usually received, but in this case she saw none of the usual excitement or pleasure. Instead there was a kind of intensity in the green eyes as they looked back at her.

'Yes, oh yes. Thank you very much.'

Miss Drake nodded, unclasped her hands and consulted the list before her. 'Good. In that case you will be notified shortly of when you are to report for duty on Casualty.'

For a moment Gemma stared at the immaculate figure opposite, feeling a numbing disappointment creep over her. 'Y-you did say Casualty?'

Miss Drake beamed. 'Yes, as it happens you're very lucky. We wouldn't normally have had a post to offer you quite so soon, but Staff Nurse Lytton is leaving to move to Scotland and we have to make up someone to take her place. You'll have spent some time in the department during your training, of course?'

Gemma sat in a kind of numbed state of disappointment. 'Yes. I did two months there.' And hated every minute of it, she thought. Of all the places she had least allowed to figure in her speculations, Casualty had been it. Oh, she knew some nurses loved it, preferred the speed with which patients came and went which allowed for no personal involvement. But that was the one thing she looked for more than anything else, the challenge, the need to drive herself on.

There was an uncomfortable tightness in her chest as she stared at Miss Drake. 'But . . . I thought, *hoped* perhaps for a surgical ward, or Women's Medical.'

The DNS's smile faded suddenly to be replaced by a look of cold reproach.

'Really, Nurse? And why exactly do you feel that you, of all my nurses, should be given the special privilege of choice?'

Gemma flinched. 'Oh, but it wasn't that. I . . .'

'I'm sure you know perfectly well, Nurse, that the policy of this hospital is to place nurses where they can be most useful and not where it suits them to be. Perhaps I should remind you that you aren't the only nurse to have gained State Registration.'

'No, Miss Drake.' Gemma swallowed hard, feeling the angry tears pricking at her eyes as she rose to her feet. 'I'm sorry. I understand.'

The DNS nodded a clear dismissal. 'I'm glad to hear it, Nurse. You will be told when you are to report. That will be all.'

Gemma walked out of the office stiff-backed and shaking, unaware of the thoughtful stare which followed her before Miss Drake sighed and returned to her work. It was ironic that, in a way, she could identify with the girl who had just left. She knew something of the tragedy Gemma had gone through, had watched her coping with it during the period of her training, not through mere idle curiosity but because she had felt a similar motivation herself a very long time ago. It was something that not many of those friends and colleagues who imagined they knew her so well over a period of some thirty years would ever be aware of.

Miss Drake's hand tightened on the pen she was holding. A hand bare of any ring, although once there had been a diamond. Until the day she had received the telegram which had told her, quite simply and without emotion, that the man she was to have married had been killed in action during his very first week in the trenches. She stared out of the window. She had great hopes for Staff Nurse Lawson, provided she could come to terms with the battle which was still so obviously going on inside her pretty head.

Gemma walked back to the ward in a daze. It was some seconds before she realised she had actually passed the senior registrar or that he had murmured a curt, 'Good morning,' before walking on, engrossed in conversation with his colleagues. But not so engrossed, she thought, that he hadn't seen the totally blank look she had cast in his direction. For some reason she felt irrationally cross with herself and turned round, an apology on her lips, but it was too late—and in any case it hardly mattered, she told herself, watching the tall figure stride away. He probably didn't even recognise me, she thought. It was definitely turning out to be one of those days.

It was a relief to find herself suddenly released to go to lunch. Anne Hayward had reached the cafeteria first and waved from where she was keeping a place at one of the tables.

'I was hoping you'd manage to get first lunch. How's it going? Any glorious changes to report since you got your stripes, so to speak?' She paused in the act of ploughing manfully through a dish of apple pie and custard to watch Gemma toying glumly with a carrot. 'What's wrong? You look as if you just heard the world was coming to an end.'

'What? Oh, sorry—nothing really.' Gemma put her fork down. It was no good, her stomach couldn't face food. 'As a matter of fact, I had an interview with Miss Drake this morning. I've been made up to Staff.'

'But that's marvellous! We'll be able to shop

together for our new belts and dresses. When do you start? Perhaps we can arrange an off-duty together and go into town.'

Gemma stirred her coffee disconsolately, not even really aware of what she was doing. 'I'm not sure yet. As soon as the girl I'm taking over from leaves to move to Scotland.'

'Well I don't know about you, but I'm beginning to feel like a real nurse at last.' There was a look of smug satisfaction on Anne's face as she said it. 'Which ward will you be on, anyway?'

'Casualty.'

'Great, lucky you.'

Gemma's gaze rose. 'You think so?'

'Well yes, don't you?'

She drained her coffee and stared at the cup. 'To be honest, I think I shall hate it.'

'For heaven's sake why? What's wrong with it?'

Gemma shrugged. 'Nothing, I suppose. I'd just set my heart on a surgical ward or even medical. In fact I'd considered everything except Casualty, which serves me right.'

'Well at least there's plenty of variety down there. Something different every few minutes,' Anne shrugged.

'That's just it. It's the impersonality I don't like. It makes it all seem like a conveyor belt. Apart from that, everyone knows that Casualty has its mad spells when you're rushed off your feet and then perhaps hours with nothing more than the odd cut finger.'

'Yes, well some people I know would consider that a bonus.'

'I wish that's how I could look at it. Unfortunately I can't.'

'So what will you do?'

'I don't know. I don't see that I have much choice.' In fact the one good thing Gemma could say about it was that at least she wouldn't have to come into contact with Niall Barratt. The thought brought a reluctant smile back to her lips as she got up. 'I'd better get back.'

'So had I. Wait for me. I'll walk to the stairs with you.' Anne struggled to her feet and groaned. 'You must be mad wanting a surgical ward! I've only been on one for a couple of days and I feel dead already.' They paused at the door leading to the stairs. 'By the way, I take it you'll be going to the party at the weekend?'

'Party?' Gemma remembered vaguely having heard something about it. 'No, I don't think so. They're not really much in my line.'

'Oh come on, you can't not.'

'Honestly, I don't know that I'd be very good company. I haven't been to one for ages.' In fact, she reflected with some surprise, the last one had been about six months after Bill's death and it hadn't been a success. People had tried too hard to be kind, saying the right thing with such obvious embarrassment, or saying nothing at all, that she had only felt uncomfortable and had finally stopped going.

Anne studied the pale face dispassionately. 'You'll have to come out of that shell sooner or later, you know. At least you could make a pretence of enjoying it. Everyone else who qualified will be there.' She held the door open and they ran up the stairs. 'It's probably the last chance we'll get to say goodbye to some of our set before they go on to do their midder training, and at least half a dozen are leaving to go to different hospitals. One has even managed to get herself a job abroad. Oh come on, all you have to do is show your face.'

It sounded simple enough and Gemma knew she would probably regret it if she didn't say goodbye to some of the friends she had made during training.

'I suppose you're right. I haven't a thing to wear, though.'

'That's all right,' Anne grinned. 'Neither have I. What about skipping lunch one day and dashing into town? Tomorrow?'

Gemma found herself back on the ward, her head in a whirl and acknowledging just the tiniest twinge of excitement. After all, Anne was right, it couldn't do any harm. All the same, she went back to work wondering what on earth she had got herself into and knew she was probably going to end up regretting her decision before the weekend arrived.

# CHAPTER FIVE

WATCHING the toast browning under the grill as she
made herself a snack that evening, Gemma went
over the interview with Miss Drake again and
speculated wearily on whether perhaps there
wasn't something to be said after all for moving on
to do her midwifery training. It would certainly
present a new challenge. On the other hand, it
would also upset all the plans she had made, the
personal belief she had always held about gaining
experience at a senior level on the wards first. A
frown made its way into her brow, deepening as the
doorbell rang and she came back to reality with an
exclamation as she saw the steady cloud of smoke
which was engulfing the kitchen.

'Damn!' She blew out the flames on what had
been a piece of toast and threw the charred remains
into the bin, wincing as it burned her fingers. The
bell rang again and she switched off the gas. Now
who on earth can that be at this time of night? she
wondered.

Blowing crossly on her smarting fingers, she
flung the door open and found herself staring at the
figure standing there. 'Sue! Good heavens!'

'Sorry, I know it's a bit late . . .'

'That's all right.'

'I wondered if I could just have a chat? It doesn't
matter though, if you're busy.'

Gemma was disconcerted to see the sudden
gleam of tears and was galvanised out of her trance
and into action. She held the door open.

'Of course I'm not. Come in, it's lovely to see you. Oh lor, ignore the clouds of smoke, I was just making a snack.' She looked at the pale face and reddened eyes. 'I don't suppose you'd like something?'

Sue followed her into the sitting-room, looked about her vaguely and sat down. 'Oh no, thanks. Well, perhaps a cup of coffee if you wouldn't mind. You're sure you don't mind?'

'To tell you the truth, I'm glad of the company.' Smiling as she stood in the doorway, Gemma realised it was true. She hadn't really wanted to eat anyway; it had been something to do, to take her mind off other things. 'I wouldn't mind a chat myself. It beats talking to yourself.' She saw Sue's faint attempt at a smile in response and said brightly, 'Look, I'll just go and make the coffee and rustle up some biscuits. You make yourself comfy.'

From the kitchen she called out, 'It's been ages. How come you're not on duty? And if you're not on duty, where's that gorgeous husband of yours?'

The instant she had said it, Gemma could have bitten her tongue out as she heard the loud sniff. She returned bearing cups and just in time to see Sue blowing her nose and scrabbling about frantically in her bag for more tissues.

She put the cups down and pushed a box towards her. 'Here, help yourself to these. I always keep a supply handy.'

'It's my night off.' Sue took a handful and smiled weakly. 'As for Dick, well to be honest, I'm not sure. The only thing I know is that he left a note.' She pulled it from her pocket, gulped hard and handed it to Gemma. 'He says he's fed up of having a wife who's never home and . . . who never finds the time even to share his bed.'

Another stream of tissues left the box and Gemma felt her heart contract as the crumpled note was thrust into her hand. She stared at it, recognising Dick's scrawl, and wondered in a moment of bleak humour why doctors' handwriting was always illegible. Her eyes skipped over the words, making her feel as if she was an intruder. *We both know we can't go on like this. I love you but I want a proper marriage, a wife who is at home just occasionally when I am . . .*

Gemma dragged her gaze away. She couldn't read any more. 'I'm sure he doesn't mean it. Have you any idea where he's gone, anyway?'

Sue reached for her coffee, hands shaking as she sipped at it, trying to regain something of her composure.

'That's the trouble, I think he does mean it. He's talked about walking out before, you see, unless things changed. But what can I do?' She lowered her head, pressing a hand to her mouth. 'I love him too, but he doesn't seem to realise that I can't throw up my job, leave, just like that. How can I? And besides, doesn't what I want matter too?'

Gemma stared helplessly at the distraught figure and remembered Dick Foster's own stricken face when he had spoken to her that morning. She had recognised a kind of desperation but she hadn't imagined it would lead to this. It all seemed so crazy, that two people who obviously loved each other could hurt each other so much. She bit her lip. 'What will you do?'

'I don't know.' Sue looked up at her, then stared into her cup. 'What can I do? I've worked hard too, you know. Nursing means a lot to me. I worked hard to qualify.'

'More than your marriage?' Gemma saw the painful drawing together of her friend's brows and regretted the question. The answer was never that simple. She shook her head and tried to force a note of lightness into her voice. 'Look, I'm sure you'll find it doesn't mean anything. Everyone says things they don't mean. He's probably had a hard day and is back at the flat biting his nails and waiting for you to arrive home right now. I'm sure it will all blow over.'

'No it won't,' Sue retaliated forcibly. 'We've been leading up to it for a long time. These past few weeks have been hell.' She put her cup down. 'I don't know what I'm going to do. His mother rang to see if we're going over next weekend or not, but I can't. I really have tried everything to change shifts. I swore I wouldn't because I know how unfair it is.' She laughed wryly. 'Not that it did me much good, anyway. We're only just managing to cover as it is.'

'I take it you've explained to Dick?'

'I've tried. It hasn't really made any difference. In fact I think it's even worse, as if it's all my fault.' Sue got to her feet. 'I'm sorry, I really didn't mean to burden you with it. I'm tired and mixed up and I don't fancy having to go back to an empty flat. Not yet, anyway.'

Gemma bit her lip and came to a decision. 'Well, there's no need for that. You're welcome to stay here for the night, if it will help.'

The relief on Sue's face was all too evident, even though it left Gemma with an awkward feeling that perhaps she had done the wrong thing. She pushed the thought away.

'The spare room is a bit small but I expect it will do. I'll find some blankets.' She paused in the doorway. 'Even so, don't you think you'll have to get together with Dick sooner or later and try to sort things out?'

'Unfortunately, getting together seems to be our worst problem,' Sue laughed wearily. 'We have tried. We just seem to end up arguing. Look, I really am sorry to involve you. I know it isn't fair. I just didn't know what else to do or who else to go to.'

No, it wasn't fair, Gemma decided crossly, having made up the bed in the spare room, seen her friend settled and finally made her way to her own bed at last. She lay for a long time staring at the ceiling, plumping her pillows and still not able to sleep. Dividing her loyalties between two people, both of whom she considered good friends, was not something she relished. Nor was getting up at six o'clock and having to go on duty without having had any sleep. She punched her pillow again, turned on her side and heard her stomach rumble. And furthermore, she hadn't had any supper either . . .

# CHAPTER SIX

GEMMA LEFT for the hospital without seeing Sue next morning. She tapped lightly on the bathroom door as she passed on her way out.

'Best of luck if you're gone before I get home tonight.' There was a muffled response which she couldn't translate and, anyway, there was no time to think about it as she headed for the car and managed to arrive on the ward just by the skin of her teeth.

She had arranged to take first lunch and had even been granted an extra half-hour to make up for having stayed late one evening, all of which made for a huge disappointment when she went for coffee only to learn that Anne wasn't going to be able to make the shopping trip after all.

'Sorry. It's just my luck,' Anne groaned. 'It's the one day Sister has to go to the dentist and she won't be back until one, so I have to take second lunch. I'd been looking forward to our shopping expedition too. Still, you could still go.'

'Oh, I don't think I'll bother. It's not quite the same, trudging round alone somehow.' But when lunch-time came, the idea of getting away for a breath of fresh air was suddenly far more appealing than going down to the crowded cafeteria, and on the spur of the moment Gemma raced out of the hospital gates, caught the local bus into town and found herself wandering among the shops, feeling her tensions gradually slipping away as she browsed and even managed to find a new dress after all. She hadn't intended buying it. The uniform had been the real purpose of her trip and that lay in the carrier bag, waiting to be taken out and gloated over the first chance she got. It was still difficult to think of herself as a staff nurse. Perhaps the reality would only hit her when she actually saw herself in the mauve dress.

She was still turning over excuses to get out of going to the party in her mind, when her eye settled on a dress in the window display of one of the larger stores. Without even giving herself time to think about it, Gemma went in and tried it on, emerging on to the street minutes later clutching a larger carrier bag and her purse, lighter by more pounds than she cared to consider.

A few rumblings in her stomach reminded her that she still hadn't eaten and she walked into a small café where she ordered coffee and a salad and sat musing with a slight frown on her face. What on earth had prompted her to buy a new dress for a party she didn't particularly want to go to anyway?

She looked up as someone jolted her arm and came to with a sense of shock as she caught a glimpse of the clock and realised, with sudden panic, that she was only just going to make the bus if she ran all the way.

In the event it made no difference. She arrived at the stop, hot and dishevelled, just in time to see it disappearing into the distance. There wouldn't be another for a least half an hour.

'Damn.' She gritted her teeth fiercely, knowing full well that even if she started walking now she was still going to be horribly late, and being late was one of the unforgivable sins.

She was standing uncertainly on the pavement, wondering which would be the lesser of several evils—to start walking, wait for the next bus or to hunt for a taxi—when a car slid to a halt in front of her. She gave it only a cursory glance, shivering as the first spots of rain began to fall, and could have kicked herself for her stupidity.

So much for my promotion to staff. It will probably be the shortest on record, she thought miserably. She clutched her carrier bag defensively closer as tears pricked threateningly under her lashes.

She had half turned, grudgingly coming to the conclusion that she had better start walking, when the car's window slid down and a figure leaned across. A familiar voice spoke her name.

'Nurse Lawson, can I offer you a lift?'

For a moment her heart leapt and she moved with a smile of relief towards the car, only to draw back with a gasp as she looked into the enigmatic features of Niall Barratt.

Oh no. It wasn't possible. The carrier bag fell from her grasp and she bent to retrieve it, knowing that her hair was wind-swept and her cheeks flushed with embarrassment. Of all people, it had to be him.

She drew back. 'No, thank you. I couldn't . . . I mean, I'm waiting for a bus. There's bound to be one along in a minute.'

For a moment his gaze flickered. It may have been amusement. It was far more likely annoyance, she thought, unable to credit the senior registrar with anything as remotely unlikely as a sense of humour.

'Then I'm afraid you're in for a disappointment. The last one left a few seconds ago and I happen to know there won't be another for some time.' His gaze followed her own and she blushed as she realised that he was probably fully aware that she had lied, and why. The mere thought of getting into that car, of having to sit beside him, filled her with a kind of confused unhappiness. It was bad enough having to see him on the wards.

The car door clicked open and she watched him unwind his great height from the driver's seat as he stepped out. 'I rather think you'd better accept my offer, unless you want to be late. As it is, you'll probably only just make it.'

It was galling to know it was true. With a little luck she might still be able to get on to the ward before Sister had time to notice she was late. She stood, biting her lip, mistrusting his smile, which had faded into a frown of impatience as he held open the door and cast a glance at the grey sky.

'We also stand a pretty good chance of getting soaked and probably catching pneumonia into the bargain unless you come to a decision fairly quickly, Nurse.'

She sent him a withering look which was apparently quite lost on him. Then she gritted her teeth and said icily, 'In that case, I'll be happy to accept your offer. There's nothing I should dislike more than to be the cause of your getting pneumonia, sir.'

The muscles in his jaw twitched ominously, but with a hand beneath her elbow he propelled her into the passenger seat, closed the door firmly and got in beside her.

'Don't worry, Nurse, I have every confidence in my ability to take care of myself. My concern is solely for you.'

She fought an overwhelming urge to slap the arrogance from his face. Instead she stubbornly refused to meet his gaze by staring purposefully out

of the window. 'In that case, please put your mind
at rest. I am perfectly capable of looking after
myself, too.'

He had already slipped the car into gear and they
had moved soundlessly into the stream of traffic
before she heard him say, softly, 'I wonder if you
are?'

Her eyes flashed indignantly as she swung towards him, taking in the sheer masculine force of
his profile as he concentrated with total unconcern
on the road ahead. There was something about the
sensuous mouth and the hard line of his jaw which
sent a violent and totally unexpected fire rushing
through her, and she pressed back into her seat,
mouth clamped into a rigid line, her hands clasped
with inexplicable nervousness in her lap. Just what
kind of man was Niall Barratt? she wondered. Was
that sensuous mouth and those large, incredibly
sensitive hands capable of human warmth, or did
nothing count beyond the sterile, whiter-than-
white coldness of his work?

She hadn't realised she was looking at him again
until he turned and reflected her gaze, bringing the
flush to her cheeks. For a moment she held her
breath, then released it slowly as she imagined for
one horrifying moment that he had actually been
able to read her thoughts.

'Relax.' His voice shattered the illusion. 'I don't
eat nurses, or whatever else it is my reputation has
been maligned with. I assure you, Nurse Lawson,
you're perfectly safe with me.'

Her mouth opened in a retort, only to close again
as she turned quickly away rather than let him see
the confusion and embarrassment in her eyes.
What on earth was the matter with her? Why
should she feel so cheated, simply because he had

snatched away the fleeting image of what it would be like to be kissed properly by such a man.

Her pulse was racing as the car finally slid to a halt and she clambered out, muttering her thanks and turning to run up the steps before he could say another word. As it happened, she was able to tidy her hair, splash cold water on to her face and appear on the ward in time to receive nothing more than Sister's meaningful glance at the clock.

She breathed a sigh of relief, not caring that it was ungracious of her to refuse to thank Mr Niall Barratt for coming to her rescue.

# CHAPTER SEVEN

SHE WOKE next morning with the awful feeling of panic which always accompanied the fear that she had overslept. It was only as she rolled over to glare at the alarm that Gemma realised it was still only six o'clock and that it was her day off. Habit died hard, but at least it was some consolation to be able to turn over again and bury herself beneath the covers. Or would have been, if she had been able to go back to sleep.

She eventually gave up the effort and lay with her hands clasped behind her head, watching the curtains moving in a slight breeze at the window, and found herself wondering if Niall Barratt was awake yet and what sort of routine he went through before beginning his day's work. He wasn't married, so there was no wife to cook his breakfast, no slippers by the fire waiting for him when he arrived home in the evening. Not that she could for one moment imagine him as a slippers-by-the-fire man . . .

She sat up quickly, drawing her knees up under the covers. What was she doing, thinking about the senior registrar anyway? What he did with his private life was no concern of hers.

She got out of bed, padded into the bathroom and out again minutes later to make coffee. She was just sitting enjoying her second cup and glancing through the morning paper when she heard a key in the lock and Sue appeared, looking tired and tense and suspiciously red around the eyes. Gemma felt her heart sink.

'Hi, you look all in. Rough night?'

'Not really. No worse than usual, anyway.' Sue shrugged herself out of her coat, tossed it aside and ran a hand through her hair. 'Is that coffee?'

'Mm. Here, I just made it.' Gemma poured an extra cup.

'I didn't think you'd be up. I was going to creep in.'

'There's no need for that. I'm usually up early anyway.'

Sue glanced at her watch. 'Aren't you going to be late?'

'It's my day off. Thank heavens!' Gemma stretched and yawned lazily.

'Lucky you.'

'Yes, well I don't know about that. I thought I'd spend it catching up on some chores and then wallowing in a hot, scented bath to see if I can't get rid of some of the ravages before the party tonight.'

'You don't sound exactly enthusiastic,' Sue yawned.

'No, I'm not. I tried all sorts of excuses, none of which convinced me. The trouble is, it's the sort of event you can't really avoid without seeming stand-offish. Still, I needn't stay long. Just enough to say my congrats and goodbyes.'

'As I remember, when I passed my finals the drink flowed pretty freely. Watch out for the punch. It looks pretty innocuous but it's usually laced with something fairly lethal!'

'Thanks for the warning. I'll stick to lemonade.' Gemma carried her cup to the sink. 'How about some breakfast? Let's be really decadent and have bacon and eggs.'

'Oh God, no.' Sue's face whitened. 'Thanks all the same, but I don't think I could face it. Toast will do fine. Tell you what, I'll make it. It will give me a chance to make myself useful.' She wandered out to the kitchen and stood hesitantly in the doorway. 'I really am grateful, you know, for letting me stay on a bit longer.'

'That's okay. I'm glad of the company.' Gemma didn't miss the forced brightness or the gleam of tears. 'I'll hunt for some bread. You see to the table.' She lit the gas and heard the crash as a plate hit the floor.

'Oh damn . . .' Sue bent to retrieve it, sniffing hard as she apologised and flung the pieces in the bin. 'Sorry.' She laughed. 'I always seem to be saying that these days. I don't know what's the matter with me. I'm not usually so clumsy.'

Gemma rescued the toast and peered in the fridge for butter. 'I don't suppose you've been in touch with Dick?'

'No. But there's hardly any point, is there?'

'I don't know. I just thought you might have had a chance to talk.'

'I don't see what there is to say. After all, he's the one who walked out and said he wouldn't be back unless things changed.'

Gemma bit back a sigh. 'I'm sure he didn't mean it. People often say things on the spur of the moment and regret it later.'

'You really think so?' Relief flickered briefly in Sue's eyes, only to fade with equal swiftness. 'In that case he knows perfectly well how to reach me when I'm on duty.'

'But you can't go on like this,' Gemma gestured helplessly. 'It all seems so . . . so futile! I know how much in love the pair of you really are. For heaven's sake, I was at your wedding.' She stopped, acutely aware that she wasn't helping, and returned to slapping butter on the toast. 'Sorry. Look, now you've got *me* at it too!' She handed over the plate and a jar of marmalade. Sue stared at it without moving.

'I don't suppose . . . I don't suppose you'll be seeing Dick?'

'No,' Gemma said, relieved that at least she was able to answer truthfully. 'But then I rarely have any reason to go down to Casually or Out-patients, you know that.'

Sue nodded bleakly. 'I just thought . . . Well, it doesn't matter anyway.' She stared at the toast again. 'I don't think I can manage this after all. I'll just have a bath and go to bed if you don't mind.'

She headed for the door and didn't look back as she said brokenly, 'If you do happen to see him, I'd rather you didn't tell him I'm here.'

The bathroom door closed and Gemma stood, disconsolately biting into her toast, wondering how she could possibly be expected to deal with other people's romantic problems when she was totally incapable of coping with her own. She perched on a bar stool, chin in hand, and gazed out of the window. Men. Why did they always have to make things so complicated?

The rest of the day vanished in an orgy of spring cleaning which had been quite unintentional until she had suddenly found herself looking at the tiny kitchen with a jaundiced eye. Before she knew it, she was emptying cupboards and attacking paint-work with the kind of energy which, happily, left no time for any other thoughts to intrude. It was late afternoon before she was brought to a halt by the telephone ringing, and it was only as she answered it that she realised she hadn't eaten and was feeling thoroughly exhausted.

A glimpse in the mirror did nothing to improve things. Her hair was escaping in wisps from the scarf she had tied round it. Her face was hot and shiny and there was a smut on her nose. Turning defiantly away, she reflected that it was just as well Niall Barratt couldn't see her now because her appearance certainly wouldn't enhance his opinion of her. Not that his opinion mattered anyway, she told herself with a vague feeling of depression, and came to earth with a bump as Anne's voice spoke in her ear.

'I thought I'd better remind you that we're all meeting at Dino's first for a drink tonight before we go on.'

Gemma frowned, stirring her memory for some recollection, and heard a low moan at the other end of the phone.

'You haven't forgotten?'

'No . . . no of course not,' she insisted quickly. 'Well, not really. I've just been up to my eyes in spring cleaning, that's all.'

'Honestly, Gemma, you really are the limit. Look, hadn't you better start getting yourself organised? You don't want to be the last to arrive at the party.'

Gemma's gaze flew guiltily to the clock and she gasped disbelievingly. It couldn't be. It wasn't possible. But her watch only confirmed it and she swallowed a tiny feeling of panic. 'Look, don't worry, I'll make it. There's plenty of time.'

'Yes, well I hope so, because I asked Nick Barnes, one of the housemen on Casualty, to arrange a lift for you.'

'There was no need.' Gemma was already struggling to untie the headscarf and muttered as a finger-nail broke. 'I could easily get there under my own steam.'

'Yes, I know. But if the offer's there, why refuse it? There's no sense taking two cars when one will do.'

Gemma sighed, seeing all her hopes of being able to beat an early and hopefully unnoticed retreat vanishing rapidly into thin air.

'Anyway, I'd better go. I have to get to the hairdresser's.'

'Wait,' Gemma called quickly, before the receiver could be put down. 'What will you be wearing?'

'Oh, something fairly sexy. After all, a girl has to make the most of her chances. All those beautiful young doctors!'

Gemma muttered something suitably vague and came away from the phone felling even more depressed. She wandered into the bedroom minutes later to ponder doubtfully on the dress which, until then, had seemed perfectly suitable and now looked increasingly prim and unsexy.

'Oh well,' she sighed, heading for the bathroom and a quick shower instead of the long soak she had spent the day promising herself. 'You'll just have to do.' She consoled herself with the thought that, anyway, she wasn't in the doctor-hunting stakes and that no one was likely to be in the least bit interested in what she wore.

In fact, standing in front of the mirror later, she wasn't at all displeased with what she saw. She had decided to leave her hair loose and it hung, shining attractively, against her neck. And while the full-skirted dress in its pretty shades of muted autumn rusts couldn't by any stretch of the imagination be described as sexy, it looked very nice. It was a colour which Bill had always said suited her particularly well and the thought helped to boost her morale a little as she added a final touch of colour to her lips and picked up her bag just as the door bell rang.

It occurred to her that she should have asked who her lift was to be. The thought of sitting beside a perfect stranger gave her a momentary feeling of uneasiness. She shook it off, telling herself sensibly that she knew most of the young housemen by sight anyway, and they were a pretty reasonable bunch on the whole. In any case, it wasn't as if she would have to spend an entire evening with whoever it was.

She hurried to the door, fumbling in her bag to make sure she had her keys, and smiled vaguely at the figure standing there. 'You're very prompt,' she said approvingly. 'It's just as well I was ready on time.'

He reached behind her to close the door and she turned as Niall Barratt said coolly, 'I happen to be one of those annoying people who considers punctuality to be a matter of politeness.'

Her smile faded as her gaze flew up to take in an immediate impression of the tall figure in an expensively cut, immaculate dark suit. It was crazy the way her heart began to thump wildly.

'Y . . . you?' She looked beyond him to the sleek, black car parked at the kerb and felt her cheeks flush with embarrassment. There had to be some mistake. She tried to turn back, dropped her keys and watched helplessly as he bent to retrieve them, letting them fall calmly into her hand.

'You seem surprised.'

She floundered. 'I thought . . . I thought you were my lift. He must be late after all.' She stared at her watch without really seeing it and wished heartily that the ground would open and swallow her up, but his hand was under her arm and he made no attempt to release it.

'That's right.'

She hung back. 'But you can't be!'

His dark brows drew together and he said softly, 'I'm afraid you're going to have to put up with me, Gemma. Shall we go? We don't want to be the last to arrive, do we?'

He was propelling her forward, his hand beneath her arm as he opened the car door and saw her seated comfortably inside. She was still struggling to find something to say as he sat beside her and started the engine, but her voice seemed to have deserted her. What must he think of being asked to pick her up? She found herself surreptitiously studying his profile, as if it might tell her just what was going on behind those enigmatic features. If he was furious it didn't show, but he could hardly be pleased. Niall Barratt was hardly a man who would be accustomed to having to ferry very young and very junior nurses and, the thought came to rub salt into the wound, it seemed to be becoming something of a habit in her case. Worse still, a habit she could easily get to enjoy. The thought crept traitorously into her mind and she squirmed uncomfortably in the plush seat so that he turned and said, placidly,

'Would you like to move the seat back a little to give you more leg room? There's a lever just down by your feet.'

Blushing furiously she reached for it, even though there was ample room as it was, but anything was preferable to having him see her embarrassment.

'I'm awfully sorry you were put to this trouble,' she said at last, almost choking on the words. 'There was really no need. I could quite easily have driven myself.'

He didn't disturb his concentration by turning to look at her, but she saw the fractional movement of his brows. 'I'm sure you could.' He glanced in his side mirror and the car purred effortlessly forward. 'But since I was going anyway, it would have been a little pointless. Unless of course you would rather, for some reason, I hadn't?'

He looked at her directly this time and Gemma felt her heart perform an odd little somersault. The Niall Barratt she was looking at now, in the dark suit and white shirt which seemed to emphasize his tan, was a far different figure from the one she was accustomed to see on the wards. Disturbingly different. She looked away quickly as she realised she had been staring, and muttered quickly,

'No, of course not.' She felt glad that his gaze was back on the road and he hadn't noticed the colour staining her cheeks. 'I just didn't want you to think that I . . . that I arranged it, that's all,' she added lamely.

'My dear girl, the thought didn't even cross my mind. And if it had, let me assure you that if it had been inconvenient I would certainly have refused.'

Well, that certainly puts me in my place, Gemma thought. She stared resolutely ahead, not doubting what he had said for one moment. Which, in a way, only served to make her even more confused until she decided that there was really no point in trying to fathom an enigma like Niall Barratt anyway.

She was glad to sit in silence for a while as he concentrated on his driving, leaving her free to stare out of the windows. Perhaps the dress hadn't been such a good idea after all, she thought, and jumped as he spoke.

'Why don't you relax? You look very nice. That colour suits you.' His gaze flickered with brief approval over her and away again. He was just being polite, of course, she told herself, and spent the rest of the journey wondering why it should be so important to her what he thought.

'I gather some of them are going to Dino's first for a drink. Do you want to?'

'No.' She couldn't bear it. 'That is, not really, unless you do.'

'Not particularly,' he said mildly. 'We'll go straight on then, shall we?'

Probably thinks there's safety in numbers, she thought, murmuring a response, and occupied herself by searching in her bag for a handkerchief.

The party was in full swing by the time they had parked the car and walked up the steps to where the sound of music was already blaring. The room was crowded with chattering groups and dancing figures and Gemma stood in the doorway, conscious of the sudden tension in her limbs, the blind panic which actually made her try to draw back. It all brought back too many memories, just when she had thought she was beginning to get her emotions in check. With Bill she would have gone in laughing, but not now.

Without even being aware of it, she had half turned, her eyes wide with fright as she looked for an escape—only to feel the gentle but firm pressure of Niall Barratt's hand on her arm.

'It looks as if it's going to be a bit of a crush.' The dark eyes looked directly into hers, but if he was aware of the terror she was feeling there was no sign of it as he said coolly, 'I think it might be best if I lead the way, don't you? I suppose I should have realised. These dos are always the same.'

She drew in several deep breaths in an attempt to steady her heart and released them shakily. 'I wouldn't have thought this was your kind of scene.' She saw his mouth quiver and countered quickly, 'That is, I mean . . .'

'That's quite all right. I think I know what you mean.'

Somehow she doubted it as she gazed furiously at the dancers gyrating in the centre of the floor and tried to imagine him out there.

'As it happens, I like to put in an appearance at these things.'

'Duty?' She couldn't help the faintly mocking note in her voice and regretted it again as he looked at her.

'Not duty at all. I may be old-fashioned, but I like to get to know the people I may some day work with, and this seems as good a way as any. You get to know far more about people when they unwind and behave naturally, don't you think?'

She looked away quickly. 'Yes, I suppose so. I'm sorry, I should have known.'

'Why?' He said it with an abruptness which shook her. 'You don't really know anything about me at all.' He stared at the crowd, frowning. 'As it happens, I also arranged to meet someone here.'

She realised with a sense of guilt that the thought had never even occurred to her that he might have a girlfriend. It hit her now like a wave which bore something painfully akin to jealousy, except that that would be ridiculous.

'Will you be all right?' He was looking at her and she blinked hard, nodding.

'It's the heat and the noise, I expect.'

'I know what you mean. It does rather hit you.'

Without realising it, she had allowed herself to be guided into the room and several of the people she recognised from PTS waved enthusiastically in her direction.

'Can I get you a drink?'

She shook her head, wondering miserably why he was being polite when he must want to get away to meet his girlfriend. For some inexplicable reason her eyes misted with tears and she wished he would go away, leave her alone so that she could escape.

'Gemma, so there you are! Where have you been? We've been looking everywhere for you!' A houseman she only vaguely recognised from Men's Medical grasped her in a bear-hug and a glass was thrust into her hand. She saw Anne, flushed and giggling, and the next minute Gemma found herself being drawn away into the crowd.

'Come on, let's go. We're not on duty now, so let your hair down.'

Gemma struggled to fling an apologetic glance in Niall Barratt's direction, only to find to her chagrin that she might have spared herself the effort. He hadn't even noticed. He was already deeply engrossed in conversation with an attractive, petite brunette whom she had no difficulty at all in recognising as Janet Tyler, a young doctor from Gynae.

Gemma allowed herself to be led into the crowd. After that the evening became nothing more than a matter of sheer survival, helped quite remarkably, she had to admit, by two glasses of sparkling wine which she drank quickly because it tasted fairly innocuous. It wasn't until she was half-way through the third that she suddenly realised her knees felt incredibly weak.

'Let me get you another.'

Her fingers closed protectively over the glass as Ray Clifford, the young, ginger-haired houseman, tried to remove it from her grasp.

'No thanks, honestly. I really think I've had more than enough already.'

'Well at least you're smiling. You should do it more often, it suits you.' He considered her flushed face and grinned. 'You're really quite beautiful, you know that.'

She moved her head just as he lowered his, and the kiss he had intended for her lips brushed past her cheek. She felt herself becoming vaguely annoyed. The drink, the heat and fighting off Ray Clifford's clumsy attempts at seduction for the past fifteen minutes were all combining to add to a feeling of desperation. She side-stepped a pair of grasping hands and muttered through clenched teeth, 'Oh look, there's Serena. I must say goodbye to her. She's going to New Zealand, you know.'

Gemma moved away quickly, breathing hard as she headed for the crowd which had gathered around the bar, and when she glanced back she saw to her relief that Ray was already transferring his attentions elsewhere.

'Gemma!' Serena Davies greeted her with a shriek of delight. 'I thought I'd never get to you.'

'So did I!' Gemma thrust herself between the press of bodies to shake hands. 'You're really going then?'

'You'd better believe it! Off next week, out into the wild blue yonder.' Serena bubbled enthusiasm. 'You should try it.'

'Perhaps I will, one of these days.' Gemma heard herself making the appropriate responses before she managed to detach herself from the crowd, pressing the cool glass against her cheek as she walked towards the terrace.

She gasped a little as the chill of the night air hit her. She should have brought a stole. It was a long time since she had drunk so much and she felt strangely light-headed. Behind her the music had slowed, becoming more subdued as the evening wore on, and she was glad, feeling the slight throbbing in her head. Leaning against the wall she let the sounds wash over her, waiting for the familiar tug at her emotions which always came when she remembered Bill and the way they had been so engrossed in each other and their own happiness that they had scarcely been aware of anything or anyone else. But it didn't come. Perhaps the drink had had a stronger effect than she realised and had dulled her memory.

She watched moths drawn to the light from the windows and, beyond them, the anonymous figures still dancing together. Several times during the evening she had caught herself unconsciously looking for Niall Barratt and had caught glimpses of him talking and dancing, mostly with Janet Tyler who seemed to be enjoying his company. But then, why not?

She stifled a sigh. After all, doctors were human too. She tilted her head to one side, holding her glass up to the light so that she could stare into the golden, bubbling liquid. For some reason she couldn't pin-point, she found it difficult to equate the two sides of Niall Barratt. The cold, aloof figure in a white coat with the man who seemed to be able to arouse such a variety of emotions in her.

The bubbles in the glass darkened and she narrowed her gaze questioningly as she frowned at the hazy shape.

'You're drunk,' she said aloud, conscious of a painful tightness in her throat. Then she gasped as the glass was suddenly, inexplicably, removed from her fingers and Niall Barratt stood there, a disconcerting look of anger on his handsome features.

'I'd say you're probably right.' His mouth was set in a taut line as he put the glass firmly on the table and drew her out of the rain which had begun, very lightly, to fall.

She stared at the damp spots on her dress and then up at him, thinking she should say something but not quite sure what. He swore softly under his breath.

'You little idiot! Didn't you realise?'

'I won't melt,' she retaliated defiantly, if a little unsteadily. 'Besides, I hardly see that it's any concern of yours if I choose to stand in the rain.'

A pulse worked in his jaw and she felt his fingers tighten on her shoulders. 'You're right. I don't care in the least whether you get soaked to the skin. But that wasn't exactly what I was referring to.'

She frowned crossly, at a loss to understand. Then a wave of dizziness hit her and she swayed. Without a word he took her arm and she offered only token resistance as he drew her beneath the archway. She expected him to release her but he didn't. Instead the dark brows drew together as he said angrily, 'Don't you know better than to drink that stuff as if it were lemonade?'

Her mouth trembled with a sudden urge to weep. He had no right to talk to her like this. She tried, not very successfully, to wrench herself free from his grip, only to feel it tighten.

'I didn't have that many,' she insisted sullenly. 'I'm a grown woman, in case you hadn't noticed.'

The grimness of his expression confused her. 'Oh

yes, I'd noticed. I imagine Ray Clifford did too.'

'And just what is that supposed to mean?' She
flung him an icy look and saw his mouth tighten.

'I would have thought that was pretty obvious.
Or is it possible you really don't realise . . .'

Just what she was to realise she never knew
because, incredibly, she found herself in his arms
and his mouth came down on hers in a kiss so
violent that she felt as if the strength was being
drained out of her. For several seconds surprise
held her rigid and then, suddenly, she found herself
responding, her face lifting eagerly to increase the
contact as his hands caressed her and his mouth
became more demanding.

She moaned softly, conscious of feelings she had
never experienced before, not even with Bill. Their
lovemaking had been gentle, fun. This was something far different, almost primeval, frightening in
the intensity of the sensations it aroused. A tremor
of shock ran through her. What was she doing?
How could she forget, betray a memory so easily,
so willingly? She pressed her hand against his chest,
fighting him, and he released her so abruptly that
she would have fallen if he hadn't still held her. She
stared at him, feeling cold, trembling, hating to see
the taut look on his face.

'Perhaps we've both had a little too much to
drink.' His voice was hard and cold, sending a
nerve running through her, making her conscious
of some kind of pain which wasn't entirely physical.
He was breathing hard and Gemma felt sick as she
thought she read the look of contempt on his face
before he let her go.

Why, oh why had she let herself respond? But
she knew it hadn't been a matter of choice. It had
happened involuntarily, the very thing she had

sworn would never happen. 'I'm sorry.' Her voice was little more than a whisper and his mouth twisted.

'Don't worry. I don't make a habit of forcing my attentions on unwilling females. Why not take it as just my way of saying congratulations on passing your exams?'

Her own voice sounded unnatural, trapped somewhere in her throat. 'You've already said it once.'

'So I have. I'd forgotten. Anyway, isn't that what this party is all about?'

She was still shaking as he turned away and disappeared into the noisy crowd which swallowed him up. For a long time after that she just stood, wondering whether it had really happened. The pressure on her lips was enough to convince her that it had been real—as real as her own reaction.

She stood listening to the rain, watching the leaves falling into small, dead clumps against the wall, and put her arms around her own body in a kind of self-protective embrace. She had vowed after Bill that it would never happen again. Falling in love was too painful, people only got hurt. What she had forgotten to take into account was a man like Niall Barratt, but at least now she recognised the dangers and could be on her guard.

# CHAPTER EIGHT

GEMMA tugged at the new belt encircling her waist and couldn't help the tiny twinge of pride as she stared at her reflection in the mirror. Staff Nurse Lawson. The mauve dress seemed somehow to enhance the colour of her eyes; or was it the shadows underneath which did that? Her hand strayed to the ridiculous little white-frilled pillbox of a cap perched precariously on her head and she smiled. Only nurses who had passed their finals were allowed to wear them and though they were still given the choice between these and the other type, most of the more senior nurses chose the new design.

A chattering group of nurses came into the cloakroom and, with a start, she realised that if she didn't get a move on she was going to be late.

'Morning, Staff Nurse.'

'Good morning, Nurses.' Gemma paused in the corridor to draw a deep breath before making her way, pink-cheeked, heart pounding, to Rosemary Ward at last. In fact by the time she had reached the ward and faced the prospect of seeing the senior registrar again, much of the pleasure had already faded and she was frowning nervously as she walked through the swing doors.

Her eye ran approvingly over the tables already set up in the centre of the ward, awaiting the arrival of breakfast, and third year Jane Armstrong emerged from the kitchen with a tray of coloured beakers. Gemma rescued it and helped set them out, wondering whether she might have a chance to catch Sue before she went off duty.

'Has Night Sister gone off yet?'

'No, I don't think so.' Jane glanced up the ward. 'I think I saw her with Sister Mitford a few minutes ago. Probably doing the round. Have you tried the office?'

Gemma smiled. 'No. Not yet. It's not really important. I just wanted to have a word before she goes, that's all. What sort of night have you had, anyway?'

'Oh, pretty quiet on the whole.' They arranged chairs round the tables. 'I don't know why but I always feel more exhausted when nothing happens than I do if we're constantly on the go. It seems to hit me around three in the morning. Some nights I'd almost welcome an emergency.'

'Yes, I know what you mean. I never really got used to my stint on nights. It wasn't just a complete reversal of everything I'd ever known—my stomach seemed to take longest to catch up. It couldn't adjust to the idea of having dinner at midnight, somehow.'

Jane laughed. 'It's good for the waistline but that's about the only consolation. By the way, the three-hourly feeds are made up. I had time to spare so I thought I'd get on with them. They're in the fridge.'

'Fine, thanks.'

'Nurse Williams has given the six-hourly medicines out and the three-hourly feeds have been done.' Jane ticked everything off.

'Lovely,' Gemma grinned. 'I don't know why I bothered to come in!'

'Just give it half an hour and you'll find out.'

'I know. Don't spoil it. What about preps for theatre?'

'You've only got three, so far. Two for tonsillectomies, one appendicitis.'

'Oh well, it looks as if we might get an easy day too.'

'Just don't count on it,' Jane smiled. 'It's probably the lull before the storm. Congrats on the promotion, by the way. When do you move?'

'I'm not sure. Whenever the command comes from on high.'

'Well, best of luck anyway. I can't see me ever making staff.'

'Of course you will. You know the job and you're good at it.'

Jane grimaced. 'If that was all there was to it I wouldn't be quite so worried. The trouble is, I've never been particularly good at putting things down on paper and I'm dreading the finals.'

Gemma knew the feeling. 'You can only do your best. The thing is not to panic. Read the papers carefully and remember what you've been taught on the wards.'

'Yes, well I'll try—but I know my mind will go completely blank the minute they put the paper in front of me.' She hitched up the hem of her apron. 'By the way, I have the phone number for Baby Crawford's parents here. It wasn't put on the Kardex for some reason. I expect they were in too much of a flap when he was brought in.'

'He's the little one with croup, isn't he? How's he doing?'

'Much better. I thought you might want to ring and let them know. The mother wasn't much more than a kid herself and worried sick.'

'Fine, I'll call as soon as breakfasts are over.'

Gemma scribbled the number on her own apron and smiled. 'But I dare say they'll ring the ward first.'

'Oh, there's Sister. Didn't you want to see her?'

Gemma turned and looked puzzled. 'But I thought Sister Foster was on last night?'

Jane looked up absently from the fluids chart she was filling in. 'What? Oh yes, I think she should have been. I'm not sure what happened. Perhaps she's not well or something. All I know is that Sister Fields came over from Abbey because we didn't have any senior cover.' She stifled a yawn behind the chart. 'I wouldn't mind a night off myself. Still, with a bit of luck I may get off on time. I'll go and see Sister. Take care.' With a wave she was gone, leaving Gemma to make her way slowly towards the office, a vague knot of tension gathering in her stomach.

'Good morning, Staff.' Sister's eye ran approvingly over the neat mauve uniform. 'We're a little late this morning. I gather Sister Foster didn't report for duty.' She clucked her faint annoyance. 'I must say I would have expected a little more consideration from someone who knows the difficulties it causes when senior staff have to be transferred from another ward to cover.'

'It's certainly not like her, Sister,' Gemma frowned. It wasn't like Sue at all. More to the point, if she had been ill surely she would have been at the flat—and if she wasn't at the flat, where had she spent the night? Gemma smiled with slightly wavering confidence and made a mental note to ring the flat at lunch-time. 'I expect she'll be in tonight.'

'Yes, well I hope so.' Sister unclipped her pen and glanced at the clock. 'Let's get on with the report, shall we, or we'll spend the rest of the day catching up on ourselves.'

Day staff emerged from the office ten minutes later having gone through details of each patient's condition, been allotted their various duties and each member of staff allocated the particular patients she would be responsible for during the day. The familiar routine got under way and Gemma pushed everything else firmly from her mind.

I'm probably worrying for nothing, anyway, she thought crossly. She's probably gone home to talk things over with Dick. At least, she *hoped* that was the explanation.

The breakfast trolley was wheeled in and those patients who weren't confined to bed ate at the tables in the centre of the ward while others were made comfortable at bed-tables and the very tiny ones were spoon-fed. Two babies, still on three-hourly feeds, were given their bottles and when breakfast had finally been cleared, Gemma went round with the medicine trolley. By sheer will power she managed to keep from glancing at the clock as the time for the morning round drew nearer, but it didn't stop her heart thudding every time a white-coated figure appeared through the doors.

It was ridiculous, she told herself with a flash of irritation as she sped in hot pursuit of a three-year-old who had taken it into his head to go walkabout. Last night's kiss had been the result of too much champagne. He had said himself they had both had too much to drink. All the same, the memory brought the colour flooding back to her cheeks and with it, the brief but inescapable truth that she had actually enjoyed it.

She caught a glimpse of her face in the small mirror Sister kept propped on top of the filing cabinet and experienced a slight shock at the reflection staring back at her. Her eyes looked dark and large. She brushed a hand weakly against her forehead, hoping no one would choose that minute to come into the office. It was a long time since her emotions had been in such turmoil and it wasn't a sensation she liked.

It was almost a relief when the telephone began to ring.

'Rosemary Ward. Staff Nurse Lawson speaking.' Her hand shook as she answered it, yet she was surprised to hear her voice sounding quite normal. 'Yes, we'd like the results of the biopsy this morning, please. Mr Barratt is sure to want to study them when he does his round.' Replacing the receiver she went in search of Sister. 'The results of Andy Collins' biopsy are through, Sister. I said we'd like them sent up so that they could go in with the case notes this morning.'

'Jolly good. Let's hope the news is good.' Sister turned over the infant she was changing and looked at her watch. 'You can go for first coffee if you like, Staff. We're reasonably quiet at the moment but I may be glad of you later. The round has been cancelled until this afternoon for some reason.'

Gemma's heart sank after a tantalising moment of hope. So she hadn't escaped after all. She made her way to the nurses' lounge, drank her coffee with little enthusiasm and went straight back to the ward where the rest of the morning passed quickly, leaving precious little time for anything but the job in hand.

The patients down for theatre came back to the ward and were recovering well. Gemma smiled as she watched the youngest stir, moaning a little before he stuck his thumb in his mouth and went to sleep again. She brushed the blond hair back from his face before writing the notes up on the chart and looked up as Sister came to her side.

'How is he?'

Gemma smiled. 'Another couple of hours and he'll be demanding his ice-cream.'

'Well, he's better off without those tonsils, that's for sure. I think I'll go for lunch now. We seem to be pretty well organised and I'd like to get back fairly quickly. I promised to see the Dawsons.'

'Oh yes. What will you tell them?' Gemma's dark brown eyes softened.

'What can I tell them? Their child has leukaemia but that doesn't mean we can't do anything. We can do a great deal, not least to see that they get all the help available.' Sister Mitford's shrewd gaze interpreted the look in Gemma's eyes. 'It doesn't get any easier, does it?'

'I must admit, it's the one part of the job I really hate, and with children it's far worse.'

'Yes of course it is.' They walked down the ward together. 'Unfortunately there is no real training to teach you how to deal with it. Oh yes, you receive counselling and these days it is very enlightened.'

'It still sometimes seems pitifully inadequate.'

Sister nodded. 'I think most people imagine we become immune after a while. It isn't true, of course. The death of a patient, and in particular a child, as you say, hits us as hard as anyone. We simply have to learn to control our emotions, but that doesn't mean shutting them off completely.' Her mouth formed a slight smile. 'No nurse should be ashamed to cry. I've done it myself before now. Tears can help. They remind us we're still human.'

Gemma watched the homely figure bustle away, then gathered herself briskly and headed for the sluice. Leaving Rosemary Ward may have its compensations but with so much to do this was hardly the time to stand considering them.

Lunches were served and cleared by the time Sister returned and Gemma was finally free to go for her own meal. Not that she felt in the least bit hungry as she joined the inevitable queue and came away with a tray laden with roast beef and two veg and a dish of apple crumble and custard. But habit died hard and she managed to make herself eat at least something before returning to the ward and the peaceful spot in the day when smaller patients were encouraged to take a nap before doctors' rounds and the arrival of visitors.

She had just finished a routine check of the post-op patients when Sister caught up with her, preceded by a pale young woman, scarcely more than her own age, Gemma thought, and a man who was obviously her husband who supported her gently.

'Ah, Staff, take over the ward round for me will you? I'm going to take Mr and Mrs Dawson into the office for a chat. Would you deal with any calls, too?'

Gemma schooled her features into a smile but a spasm of intense sadness still ran through her for the couple who seemed so young to have to face such a tragedy. 'Yes, of course, Sister. Shall I ask nurse to bring in a tray of tea?'

'I'm sure that would be very much appreciated. Make it three cups, will you? I could do with one myself.'

'Yes, Sister. Oh, and Sister, Radiography still haven't sent up those X-rays we were waiting for and Mr Barratt particularly asked for them. I know they're busy . . .'

'Get on to them all the same, will you, Staff.' Sister turned, then paused, frowning. 'Oh yes, that reminds me. I forgot to mention that Mr Reynolds is back so he'll be taking the rounds again from now on.' She smiled wryly. 'I don't suppose Mr Barratt will be at all sorry to get back to his own work, but I'm sure we're going to miss him.'

Gemma's mouth suddenly felt dry. 'I don't . . . I don't understand, Sister. Mr Barratt leaving?'

'Well it *was* only a temporary arrangement. Mr Reynolds was lucky to find someone like Mr Barratt, with a general surgical background, willing to take over for him while he took an extended leave. But his particular interest is orthopaedic surgery so I suppose we musn't blame him for being glad to get back to it.' Sister looked at her watch and at the young couple being ushered into her office by one of the junior nurses. 'I really would have liked to be on the ward myself, as it's Mr Reynolds' first day back. There are bound to be several queries.'

'I'm sure I'll be able to cope, Sister.' Gemma offered the reassurance despite the fact that, inside, she was far from calm. Shaking in fact. It didn't make sense. She should be pleased, yet perversely she felt cheated. She had steeled herself for a confrontation which, it struck her now, he must have known would never come.

She brushed a hand against her eyes as the doors opened and she began to walk mechanically towards them, case notes in her hand. Perhaps she should be grateful, the thought intruded, and her chin rose. After all, he had done nothing more than remind her of a promise she had made to herself a long time ago, that she wasn't going to get involved with any man ever again.

So why was it all going wrong? a devilish little voice asked. Why was it that, try as she would, somehow Niall Barratt kept forcing his way into her life, even into her thoughts—and with such devastating effect, too.

She stared bleakly ahead. No answer seemed to offer itself except one which she refused even to contemplate. She was not falling in love. Love made you vulnerable and she had no intention of laying herself open to that kind of pain again. It was easy to say, but for the rest of the day she felt tired and miserable, as if a cloud hung over her head, refusing to be dispersed.

# CHAPTER NINE

IT WAS late when she got back to the flat feeling both mentally and physically battered. For once she didn't even bother to make anything to eat but had a bath and slipped into bed, to fall into a heavy sleep. But next morning she awoke exhausted and hollow-eyed and received the inevitable lecture from Sister Roberts, who was well known for being a strict disciplinarian.

'You're looking peaky, Nurse. Not the result of too many late nights, I hope. I shouldn't have to tell you, of all people, about the duty of a nurse to keep herself fit and mentally alert. This job makes a great many demands upon a girl.' She pronounced it 'gairl' and Gemma cringed, feeling like a raw probationer. She began a vigorous sifting through the filing trolley, trying to shut the words out.

Miss Roberts was one of the old school and Gemma found herself wondering, as she fixed her gaze at some point beyond the steel grey hair and wavering cap, whether Emily Roberts had ever transgressed even the most minor of hospital rules since the day she had first put on the uniform. It seemed highly unlikely.

Gemma muttered some vaguely appropriate response and added, 'I'm due for two days off this weekend, Sister.'

'Good. Well just make the most of it. Plenty of fresh air.'

Gemma abandoned a fruitless search of the

record file and frowned. 'Jemila Patel's notes are definitely not here.'

'In that case perhaps you'd better have a word with Nurse Hunter. Her idea of the alphabet bears amazingly little resemblance to the one I learned at school.'

Gemma bit her lip. 'Mm. Maybe I should try under M.'

'M?'

'Miscellaneous?'

Emily Roberts eyed her disparagingly as she rose to her feet, consulting her watch. 'Nothing would surprise me. Oh, by the way, before I forget, you're to report to Casualty when you get back after the weekend.'

Gemma felt her stomach plunge. 'So soon?'

'What's the matter? You don't look particularly pleased.'

'No, well I'd rather hoped for a surgical ward.'

'Did you indeed!' Sister snorted. 'Well I'm sure it would be very nice to choose, but we aren't free spirits, Staff Nurse. We are here to serve.'

She makes it sound like a nunnery, Gemma thought, and muttered rebelliously, 'Yes, Sister,' before turning back to the file and resuming what she guessed was going to be a useless search.

The rest of the day passed with its usual quota of drama. All the patients down from theatre seemed to be recovering nicely until one carroty-haired nine year old who had had a tonsillectomy began to bleed again.

'It's always the same.' Sister was quickly into the action. 'Always the redheads.'

The ward bustled, then quietened again as the lunch trolley arrived. Gemma found herself deftly fielding the remarks which accompanied it.

'Yuk, I can't eat this, Staff!'

She glared from Shane Williams' cheeky face to the plate of beef stew and had to admit it wasn't exactly appealing to the eye. 'Nonsense. I might have known you would find something to complain about. And just what is it that doesn't suit today?'

'Well, just look at it.' He thrust the plate under her nose. 'There's a thing floating in it.'

'A thing?' She peered into the mass of gravy and he jabbed a finger at a dark object.'

'I reckon it's a beetle.'

'A beetle? Nonsense.' She felt her stomach heave. 'Here, let me see.' She took the plate, prodded the offending item with a fork and shuddered violently as it emerged. For a second she had to close her eyes, then she made a grab at the escaping giggler and thrust the plate back into his shaking hands, minus the plastic cockroach which she held at arm's distance.

'You villain, Shane Williams!' Her voice was shrill with shock as much as laughter. The thing looked so hideously real. 'Just you thank your lucky stars I don't make you eat it.'

'Go on,' his grin spread from ear to ear, 'admit it, you thought it was a real 'un.'

'No such thing.' Gemma bristled and shuddered again as she extricated the creature from the fork and dropped it hastily into his outstretched palm. 'Just where do you get these revolting things?'

'Me mam brought it. She's gonna get me a tarantula next time.'

'Oh *really*.' Gemma made a mental note to have words with Mrs Williams.

'Yeah.' Shane was ecstatic. 'But what I really want is a Dracula mask.'

Gemma's eyebrows rose. 'But Shane, dear, you

don't need one!' She giggled and ran, until she caught Sister's disapproving eye and slowed to a walk, thinking, 'And that's another black mark, I suppose.' But for once she didn't really care.

She was definitely going to miss Rosemary Ward. The thought hit her with a depressing suddenness as she said her goodbyes and went off duty that night. But perhaps in a way Sister Mitford had been right. She did need a change. At least on Casualty she wasn't likely to keep running into Niall Barratt, though the thought seemed to offer remarkably little comfort.

Out-patients was already crowded and smelled of damp clothes and central heating as Gemma walked through Reception, passing rows of chairs and patients who stared hopefully in her direction, only to lose interest as she smiled and walked on.

Casualty was one of the older sections of the hospital and its size had somehow never seemed to increase in proportion to the demands made upon it. An ambulance drew up now and she skipped aside, holding back the swing doors as a nurse hurried to help. The patient was a child.

'Knocked off her bike on her way to school,' Gemma heard the ambulance driver pass on the information.

She made her way through the hall which housed facilities both for OP and Casualty, where the two inter-linked. She passed the door marked *Plaster*, another, *Records*, and eventually found the one bearing *Sister*. It was empty, which wasn't entirely surprising since Casualty seemed to be into the first of the day's rushes and no nurse had time to sit in her office dealing with paperwork. That was to be fitted in later during the lull one prayed for.

Gemma was just about to waylay a second year nurse who sped past bearing a steel kidney dish and a harassed look when Sister bustled towards her.

'I take it you're the reinforcement?'

'That's right, Sister.'

'Oh well, I suppose if we can't have the cavalry we must settle for one trooper, though heaven knows what they think we are down here! We're always under-staffed and no one seems to care.'

Gemma recognised the cry as one familiar to all ward sisters and met the wry gleam in Sister Ferguson's eye with one of sympathy.

'Never mind, it can't be helped. We're grateful for all the help we can get.' She popped a pen into her pocket. 'You'd better follow me.' She was already on her way, a trim, attractive figure in a navy blue dress and with black-stockinged legs which managed to look good even in the sensible flat shoes. Gemma scuttled after her.

'I'll give you a quick tour round. Show you some of the cubby-holes where we hide things and introduce you to a few names you should know. That's sterile dressings.' She swept past a door which opened to emit wafts of antiseptic as a probationer smiled and sped away. 'Examination cubicles over there. Six of them.'

Gemma's gaze took in the curtained areas, half of them already in use, and a small child, held in the arms of a white-faced woman who was pressing a blood-stained tea-towel to his mouth, being ushered into a fourth.

'That looks like a job for a few stitches. The treatment room is through there. Oh, and that's Mr Pawley, Senior Surgical Registrar. If I were you I'd resist the urge to make any kind of joke about his name. He's heard them all at least a million times.'

Sister smiled, emphasising an attractive face which seemed to have been made to model the jaunty frilled cap. 'Minor Ops is here. You'll probably see the Casualty Officer, Mike Clifton, this morning. There's no point trying to remember all the names. You'll get used to them gradually.'

Gemma wasn't so sure. There were people hurrying in all different directions and, as if she read her thoughts, Sister smiled.

'Don't worry about it. I know it all looks a bit like an ants' nest when you first come down here, but it's pretty organised chaos really and we've never actually mislaid anyone yet.'

'I hope I don't start a precedent,' Gemma said, half-jokingly.

'You'll be fine.' They paused at the desk. 'I gather you've only just been made up to Staff.'

'Yes, I'm afraid so, and I gather this is only a temporary placing.'

'Yes, I wasn't too happy about that. I like to have nurses who stay long enough to get to know what's going on. Still, it can't be helped and we all have to start somewhere. I suppose you've done some time on Casualty and OP?'

'Only briefly, during training.'

'Yes, well things don't change much. I dare say you'll even see some familiar faces on your way around, especially in OP. We tend to get the occasional down and out who slips in for a warm. They're usually quite harmless but with the best will in the world we aren't a hostel.'

'How do you deal with it?'

'Mostly they leave when asked without any trouble. If you do get one who wants to make an issue of it, don't try to tackle it alone. Get some male help and, if you have to, send for the police.

They deal with it all very quietly and we rarely get any real problem.'

'I'll remember that.'

'I'm afraid you may find yourself doing duty in OP as well, on days when they're particularly busy. I know we are supposed to be two completely separate departments, but if we have a lull and they are up to their eyes in it we usually send someone across to help with the clinics. Well, I think that's about it, or at least as much as there's any point in my telling you now.'

Gemma thought so too. Her brain was already reeling.

'It's my half-day today so I'm officially off at one, but there's a senior Staff Nurse, Jane Stuart, on duty so she'll be around to help you find your feet . . .'

'I can't imagine I'll ever get used to it,' Gemma said.

'You'd be surprised. I felt just the same when I first started, but give it a week and you'll feel as if you've been here all your life.'

A feeling which Gemma found herself in hearty agreement with when her first weekend off arrived, to be greeted with more than usual relish. The week had flown and, looking back, it seemed like one hectic round of cuts, burns, stitches and the more serious road accident victims who were rushed through to receive the intensified care the other units could offer.

By the time Friday night came she felt as if her feet had scarcely touched the ground. And Sister Black had been right; she did feel as if she had been there for ever. But there was something she found particularly soul-destroying in the speed of it all as patients came and went or were passed on with too

little time ever to know them as individuals. In fact
the only consolation, she thought as she let herself
into the flat, was that she hadn't caught even so
much as a glimpse of Niall Barratt . . .

# CHAPTER TEN

GEMMA CAME out of a brown study to find a familiar face staring at her with a certain amount of anxiety. She blinked hard.

'Sue. Oh lor, I'm sorry, I was miles away.' Back in bed in fact, she thought, thinking wistfully of the weekend which had seemed far too short.

'I should think so too. I was about to resort to sign language. Anyway, why aren't you rushed off your feet? There's a crazy rumour circulating that Casualty never sleeps.'

'It doesn't.' Gemma stifled a yawn behind her hand, keeping a wary eye out for Sister. 'But I do, occasionally. I feel dead. I seem to have spent the weekend catching up on chores. Anyway, where have you been? What's happened? I heard you'd gone off sick.'

'Oh yes, that.' Sue grimaced. 'Sorry. I feel rotten about it. Actually I didn't feel too good so I decided I might as well go home.' She saw the look in Gemma's eyes and said quickly, 'He wasn't there, at least not the first couple of nights. I gather he spent them on a camp bed somewhere. To be honest, I didn't feel in any mood to ask. What about you, anyway?'

'Oh, not too bad. I miss Rosemary. This is all too impersonal for me, too quick. I liked the involvement.'

'Yes, I know what you mean.'

'We're having a lull at the moment, just in case you get the idea that this is all we do. The early

morning accidents have gone, it's too early for the
pubs and we're shortly coming up to the infants
with their heads in saucepans. I wouldn't have
believed it until I came here! Some of the things
they get up to are positively ingenious. You
wouldn't believe it possible.'

'My dear girl, don't you know by now that impossible is a word children don't understand? I
would have thought Rosemary would have taught
you that.'

'Well I certainly do now.' Gemma dropped a file
back into place in the trolley. 'What are you doing
here anyway? This isn't normally your time or your
territory.' She hesitated. 'You weren't looking for
Dick, were you?'

A faint hint of misery crept into Sue's eyes. 'No,
not particularly. Why, have you seen him around?'

'Actually, no I haven't. In fact our paths haven't
crossed at all yet. He does come into Casualty of
course, but to be honest, for the first week I didn't
notice a soul. I think he's probably over on OP.
There's a gynae clinic this morning.'

'Yes I know.' Sue looked away. 'As a matter of
fact I didn't come looking for Dick. I've been to see
the DNS, to see if there's any chance of my going on
to days instead.'

'And is there?'

'My request has been noted, as they say. But you
know how it is. It means finding a replacement etc.,
etc.' She shrugged. 'Let's just say I was left with the
impression that it would cause a great deal of
inconvenience and probably wouldn't happen.'

'But at least Dick must see you're willing to try
and do something.'

'Oh, I'm sure he is, if he cares to think about it.
But we haven't actually discussed it and I don't see

much point in trying until I can say something definite.'

'Oh, I see.'

Sue grinned. 'It's like one of those awful never-ending sagas, isn't it? Except that I'm not at all sure this one will have a happy ending. Things are very definitely strained, you might say.'

Gemma made some sympathetic response and caught Sister's eye on her. 'Look, I'll have to go. Perhaps we can meet up for a coffee some time.'

'Fine. I'll get in touch.'

Sue left and there was the sound of an ambulance arriving. The doors opened.

'Staff, cubicle three.' Sister went to meet the stretcher. 'And have Mr Pawley bleeped, will you? We have a head injury coming in which is going to need his attention from the sound of it.'

The lull was over. The machine roared into life again and for the next two hours they didn't stop.

'Right,' Sister said, having satisfied herself that the hall really was, temporarily at least, cleared of patients. 'Nurse Reed, shoot off for coffee now and take Dixon with you. Don't be too long. I can't believe this is any more than the calm before the storm.'

They disappeared quickly, before she could be proved right, and Gemma set about renewing the dressings trolley.

'Can you cope here, Staff, if I whizz off as well for half an hour? There's a unit meeting but I should be back in time for you to go to early lunch.'

'Yes of course.' Gemma smiled. A week of Casualty had done something towards reinforcing her confidence, even if it hadn't changed her views. She was sitting at the desk writing up the casualty book when Libby Dawson, the third-year, came in muttering darkly under her breath as she rolled down her sleeves.

'Something wrong?'

'You could say that.' The girl blinked through the large spectacles which added a gamine prettiness to her face. 'That's the second time this morning some infant has thrown up all over the hall. The place reeks of disinfectant. Come to think of it,' she wrinkled her nose, 'so do I!'

Gemma laughed. 'It's not exactly Christian Dior, is it?'

'Phew, you can say that again. Talking of which, did I or did I not see you with the dishy Mr Barratt the other night?'

Gemma despised the ever-ready colour which surged to her cheeks as she stabbed the top on her pen and rose quickly to her feet. 'Did you?'

'Yes, I'm sure I did. At the finals party.'

'Well yes, you may have done. He was there so I suppose it was pretty inevitable our paths would cross sooner or later.'

Libby Dawson flung her a knowing look. 'I thought the two of you looked particularly intense before you disappeared together for a while.'

'Oh, really? I can't imagine why.' Gemma fixed her concentration solidly on the accident file and frowned. 'Unless of course it was because I had a splitting headache and had to go outside for some fresh air. I'm not much good at parties.' She smiled as she closed the file and straightened up. 'Too claustrophobic for my taste.'

She could see another question forming in the girl's mind when the bleeper in her own pocket started. She reached for the phone, saying crisply, 'St Vincent's, Casualty.' Through the background

static she heard the voice of the Chief Ambulance
Officer.

'Two vehicles on their way to you now. Details
fairly skimpy but we think three, possibly four,
victims. Fire brigade was in attendance. We're not
sure whether the driver of the second vehicle has
been freed yet.'

'We'll be ready.'

Libby Dawson was waiting, all trace of laughter
gone from her face now. 'RTA?'

'That's right. On its way in now. Three, possibly
four, victims. One driver being freed by the fire
service. I'm not sure whether they've got him yet or
not. We'd better be ready in any case. Are there
enough free cubicles?'

'I think so. I'll go and check. Norton was dressing
a gashed hand but she should be just about
finished.'

'Fine.' Gemma was already on her way. 'We'd
better make sure we have plenty of sterile packs.
There may be burns as well as other injuries. Who
else have we got on?'

'Student Nurse Kingsley and third year Nurse
Harding.'

'Well we'd better put them in the picture. Oh,
and theatre had better be warned. I'll do that now.'

Five minutes later the sirens could be heard as
the ambulances drew up outside and Gemma hurried out to meet them as the stretchers were carried
in. Curtains were whisked aside and the first of the
patients was placed gently on the examination
couch when Mike Clifton hurried in, white coat
open, stethoscope dangling round his neck.
Gemma wondered fleetingly, and not for the first
time, why it was that he always looked as if he had
just been called from his bed.

There was nothing lacking in his manner, however, as she stood aside, watching as he made his examination with gentle thoroughness.

'We'd better have this sleeve cut away.' He moved to let her attend to it with a pair of suture scissors while he studied the young man lying there. 'He's lost a lot of blood. The collar-bone is dislocated.'

He bent closer, making gentle movements which drew a groan of pain from the youth. 'Mm. It could be broken. X-rays definitely, in any case.' He moved on to a gash just beneath one eye, which was bleeding profusely. 'That will need suturing. With a bit of luck it won't leave too much of a scar.' He straightened up. 'You've been pretty lucky, all things considered,' he reassured the young man gravely. 'Let's hope we can say the same for the others.'

They worked with speed and efficiency. Mike Clifton had been right. The first victim had been lucky, especially so as more details of the accident emerged. It seemed that the other car in the accident had been stolen and taken for a joy-ride by three youths who had managed to wrap it round a tree, after causing slight injury to a passing pedestrian.

The boy who had been driving the stolen car hadn't been so lucky. Going into the cubicle, Gemma was scarcely aware that it was Dick Foster who looked at her and quietly shook his head.

'Nothing we can do for this one, I'm afraid. They had to cut him out. He's badly burned. Internal injuries. I'd say he died instantly.' His mouth tightened. 'Such a damn waste. Bloody idiots.'

'He can't have been a day over seventeen.' Somehow the shock of seeing someone badly injured never lessened, Gemma thought. She had never gained the kind of hard shell which seemed to offer some nurses immunity from distress, and her throat felt tight.

'What else do we have?'

They moved on to the next cubicle where Dick looked at Mike Clifton, who shook his head. 'We just lost this one. It was touch and go when they brought him in. I thought there might be a chance but . . .' Mike brushed a hand through his hair. 'Are there any more?'

'Someone said something about a driver being trapped.' Dick looked up from the notes he was making. 'God knows what sort of shape he'll be in.'

Gemma had heard the arrival of another ambulance and gone to investigate. She returned to the cubicle now. 'The driver has just been brought in. It looks pretty bad.' She was already checking the packs of sterile gauze and dressings, watching as a junior nurse spread the sheet over the examination couch. Then the stretcher was brought in and everything became automatic.

It was nice, Gemma thought vaguely, to see Mike Clifton and Dick Foster working so well together. They seemed to anticipate each other's moves, working quickly but with compassion as they bent grimly over the deeply unconscious man.

Gemma cut along the seam of a blood-soaked trouser leg and felt her scalp tingle as she revealed the mess beneath. Dick leaned closer.

'We'd better have that cleaned up and take a proper look. I'd say the leg is pretty badly smashed.' There was silence as each bent to their individual tasks; then Mike straightened up.

'We'll have to get someone in to take a look at this. I reckon he has a broken spine. I could be wrong. It might be damage to the nerves, but we can't take any chances. Can you bleep whoever is on call, Staff?'

Gemma raced away and returned seconds later. 'Mr Pawley is on his way.' They said nothing until Mike nodded.

'Sutures here.'

Gemma was ready, standing by as he inserted each one, to cut the silk neatly. She was scarcely aware of the figure who came through the curtains until a voice said quietly, 'What's going on here? Someone for me to look at, Staff?'

Gemma stepped back, a smile flickering briefly on her face as the senior surgical registrar moved towards the couch. Peter Pawley had a reputation as a brilliant and kindly man who didn't suffer fools gladly.

'Yes, sir, I'm afraid so. The patient was involved in a road accident. Two cars collided head on. This man was one of the drivers and had to be cut free. I'm afraid he's pretty bad.'

'I see. Well, let's take a look, shall we?' The dark-suited figure moved closer. 'You might be interested in this too, Niall. You may be able to offer some useful tips. It rather looks as if it might be your particular field.'

Gemma hadn't even been aware of the other figure standing quietly to one side until he stepped forward now. 'Thanks, I'd like to be of help if I can.'

He passed her without as much as a glance in her direction and she stood mutely, seeing the dark head with its curling hair, the aquiline nose and firm jaw, and she felt her heart start thudding so crazily that she had to clasp her hands together to stop them shaking.

Her composure was barely restored when the two men straightened up.

'Mm, I'd say there's definitely a spinal injury. We'll need X-rays, of course, to see the full extent, but I think immediate transfer to the special unit, don't you?'

'I think it's the best chance he has.'

Peter Pawley smiled. 'Lucky it's open in time. Couldn't be more opportune, at least from this poor chap's point of view.' The two walked out through the curtains which Gemma whisked aside. She stood with her gaze lowered, wondering how she could ever have been crazy enough to imagine that moving from Rosemary Ward meant she wouldn't see him again.

'Thank you, Staff Nurse.'

Her gaze rose and was intercepted by a cool pair of blue eyes before he was gone, leaving her totally incapable of guessing what had been going on in his head, and with the uncomfortable thought that perhaps she didn't really want to know.

'You can go off to lunch now, Staff.' Sister popped her head round the door of the treatment room where Gemma was checking and re-ordering stocks of supplies and other equipment which needed to be replaced.

'Thank you, Sister.' She straightened up, rolled her sleeves down and took a last satisfied look at her handiwork as she stepped out into the corridor.

'I should think you'll be glad of a break. You've had quite a morning.'

'You could say that,' Gemma agreed, thinking wanly that her appetite seemed have vanished rather anyway.

'Well, you did very well.' Sister Black was always generous in her praise and Gemma felt a quick flush of pleasure as she hurried through the reception hall and across to the staff cafeteria. She was just debating whether to skip lunch altogether and go for a walk instead when Dick Foster caught up with her in the covered walk-way which was still the traditional and decidedly chilly way, in winter, between the main block and dining facilities.

'Off to lunch?'

She made a slight face. 'I was thinking about it but, to be honest, I'm not sure I could face liver casserole just at the moment.'

He laughed. 'Funny, I was just thinking the same myself. It does tend to lose its appeal, especially after a morning like this. I don't suppose you'd like to settle for coffee instead?'

'Have you any idea what it's like trying to battle your way through the queues up there?'

'We could go to the senior lounge downstairs. I don't know about you, but I could do with a bit of peace and quiet.' He looked tired and she couldn't help noticing the lines of tension round his eyes and mouth. Gemma hesitated only fractionally.

'Why not?' She pulled her cloak round her and they turned and walked back to main reception and down the stairs to the small lounge which was reserved officially for visitors needing to stay at the hospital and the senior staff and which, as a result, was usually less crowded.

'Shall we sit by the window?' He led her to two large, comfy leather chairs and put their coffee on the small table. 'It's nice to look at something other than wards every now and again. I often come down here when I want to be quiet.'

Gemma looked round at the modern decor and plants. 'It's nice. Strictly speaking, I suppose I shouldn't be here.'

'You're my guest, so don't worry. Anyway, it's nice to see you. We don't often get the chance these days, especially since Sue started working nights.' His mouth was drawn as he stirred his coffee, not even bothering to look up as several other members of staff started to drift in in chattering groups. Gemma stared hard into her own cup, trying to think of something cheerful to say.

'Night duty's a bind. I hated it myself but it's something we all have to do.' It sounded wrong and she saw his face harden.

'I suppose so. I just hadn't planned on it becoming permanent in Sue's case.' He drank his coffee and leaned forward, arms propped on his knees, and Gemma felt vaguely shocked by the bitterness in his voice. 'When did you last come over for a meal?'

'Heaven knows!' She laughed, awkwardly. 'Ages ago, but I've been pretty busy myself too, you know, what with the finals and everything.'

He looked at her directly. 'I expect you think I'm being selfish.'

Gemma swallowed hard, toying with her spoon, not knowing what to say.

'Perhaps I am,' he went on. 'But this isn't exactly how I saw married life.'

More senior staff drifted in. Gemma watched them without seeing and wondered what on earth she could possibly say. Her gaze returned to his lowered head. 'I don't suppose Sue likes it any better than you do. She hasn't exactly been her usual cheerful self lately.'

'And you think it's my fault?'

'I didn't say that. I'm not saying it's anyone's fault.' Her brows drew together. 'Oh Dick, I love you both. I hate to see you like this, but surely there has to be some solution?'

'Well if there is, I'm damned if I can find it.' He drained his cup and put it down. 'God knows, I don't think we can go on like this much longer.'

'Isn't what you're really saying that you think Sue should give up her job?' she asked quietly.

'Is that how it sounds?' He sighed. 'I do appreciate what her job means to her.'

'She's very good at it. Sue is a first rate sister and I know she would be missed. But then, I don't suppose that's any comfort, is it?'

He shook his head helplessly. 'It's a crazy sort of situation. I just want to see more of her, to spend more time together. Unfortunately, I'm not at all sure that's what Sue wants any more.'

'I'm sure you're wrong,' Gemma protested. 'I know she is as worried as you are.'

'So where do we go from here? It looks as if we've reached stalemate.'

'Isn't that giving in rather easily? I can't believe there isn't an answer. There has to be. Other doctors have married nurses.'

He smiled wryly. 'Yes, well if you think of it perhaps you'll let me know. Preferably before it's too late.'

Gemma bit her lip again, angry with herself for having become involved and for having no solution to offer for the two people who were her dearest friends. Instinctively her hand reached out and was enveloped in his.

'I'm sorry,' he said gruffly. 'I shouldn't have dragged you into this.'

'You didn't. I'm as eager as you are to see the pair of you together again. You both mean too much to me. Anyway,' she made an attempt at humour, 'it can't last for ever, you know.'

'Unfortunately we can't stay in that poky little flat for ever either. Oh, it's convenient for the hospital. That's why we took it in the first place. But it's pretty grim. It's ironic really. That's why Sue took the job on nights, so that we could save something and get a proper place.'

'I wish I could help.'

His hand tightened over hers. 'You have. Just by listening. I suppose I needed to let off steam. I hadn't quite intended it to be here or now.'

Gemma moved a strand of hair from her eyes and glanced up as someone brushed past. Her heart contracted as a look of cold disapproval swept herself and Dick before she found herself staring angrily at Niall Barratt's disappearing back.

'Oh damn,' she muttered. 'Now what do you suppose we've done to deserve that?'

Dick looked up and grinned. 'Perhaps he thinks I have designs on your virtue.'

'Oh, for heaven's sake!' She glared at him, feeling the colour in her cheeks as she scrambled hastily to her feet, wondering why it was that every time their paths crossed she seemed destined, no matter how innocently, to give the senior registrar the wrong impression.

'On the other hand,' Dick looked ruefully at his watch, 'he's probably wondering why the devil we aren't both on duty. I should have been back five minutes ago.'

'What?' Gemma gave a yelp of horror as she looked disbelievingly at her own watch. 'Oh no, it can't be.' She headed for the door, waved goodbye and then jerked to a halt as she saw two figures standing in the corridor.

Niall Barratt's eyes fixed her with a look of supercilious amusement and she raised her chin defiantly, staring purposely straight ahead as she forced herself to walk calmly past. Whatever conclusions he may have cared to draw from seeing her with Dick Foster, she absolutely refused to give him the satisfaction of thinking she was in the least concerned by his opinion, she decided rebelliously—and knew with a slight qualm of guilt that that wasn't entirely true, however much she might wish it.

# CHAPTER ELEVEN

IT WAS A bonus in the week that followed, not to have time even to think about Niall Barratt.

Staff Nurse Julie Pearson handed over a card for filing and eased an aching foot against her other leg. 'I could do with a week off. I'm definitely starting to flag.'

'Why don't you put in for some leave?' Gemma looked up from the accident report. 'We're not particularly short of staff at the moment. Come to think of it, we're pretty flush for a change.'

'Hm. No chance, unfortunately. I've already used up my quota. Two weeks in Austria and another in Scotland.' She yawned heavily. 'It seemed worth it at the time. Now I'm not so sure.'

Gemma laughed. 'I know what you mean. Winter holidays are fine but it leaves a whole lot of year still to be got through and I hate it when everyone else is going off in the summer and I'm stuck. Still, you must have some time still owing?'

'Oh sure. But I'm saving a week for Christmas. I want to go home if I can. Trouble is, I expect everyone else will have the same idea. How about you?'

Gemma pushed a strand of hair from her eyes and frowned. 'I don't know. I haven't really thought about it yet.' It wasn't exactly true. She had toyed with the idea of going to see her parents but somehow this year she fought shy of familiar routine. Perhaps it was the move from Rosemary, or the fact that the finals were safely behind her at last. She wasn't sure, but Sister Mitford's words seemed to have stuck uncomfortably in her mind. She *had* settled into a rut. A comfortable one admittedly, but was that really what she wanted?

'I may volunteer to stay on. I've worked a Christmas before, during training, and I loved it. I didn't expect to, mind. I thought everyone would be thoroughly miserable, but it wasn't like that at all. Anyway, I've no commitments so if it means someone else can go off I don't mind doing it at all.'

Sister Black came through reception escorting a young man who was clutching his elbow. 'Is there a cubicle free, Staff?'

Gemma drew the curtains quickly. 'Here, Sister.' She made him as comfortable as possible, which wasn't easy since he was in considerable pain and his coat had to be removed.

'I think we have a broken collar-bone here, Staff. We'd better get Dr Clifford to take a look. Is he around, do you know?'

'I think I saw him about five minutes ago, Sister. A child was brought in after swallowing half a bottle of his mother's tablets.'

'Oh not again.' Sister's face contorted angrily. 'When will they ever learn not to leave things within reach?' Gemma hung the patient's jacket on a peg. 'There we are, Mr Simms. Now we'll get someone to have a look at you. You'll probably have to have some X-rays, then we'll make you more comfortable.'

'I'm a bit worried about the wife, Sister. She'll be expecting me home. I haven't had a chance to let her know what's happened.'

'Well, I expect we could do that for you.'

'Would you like me to do it, Sister, when I find Dr Clifton?'

'If you would please, Staff. If you'll just give us the telephone number, Mr Simms. There . . .' She supported the elbow. 'How's that?'

He grimaced. 'Bloody painful.'

'Yes, I'm sure it is, but we'll soon get something done about it. Oh, Staff, I'm sorry to have to do it but I'm afraid I'll have to send you across to Outpatients. They seem to be a bit short and asked if we had anyone to spare. I know you haven't done a stint there yet so I'm afraid you're it.' She smiled sympathetically. 'Sorry. One of these days someone will probably devise a better system and we won't have three clinics taking place at the same time, but at the moment St Vincent's don't have it.'

Gemma smiled with a lightness she was suddenly far from feeling as they stepped out of the cubicle and she prepared to go in search of Mike Clifton. 'I'll go straight over, Sister.'

'I really do wish you didn't have to, but as you're only here on a temporary basis . . .' Sister's hand rose resignedly. 'You've fitted in very well here.'

'I've quite enjoyed it.' But as she made her way through reception to the other hall, Gemma couldn't entirely dismiss a slight feeling of discontent. She *did* like Casualty, but somehow it lacked the special something she had always experienced on the wards, the feeling at the end of the day that she was actually involved.

'I feel like a general dogsbody,' she muttered to no one in particular as she walked through the doors and glanced desperately at the rows of damp, dejected figures who turned to look in her direction with a momentary gleam of pleasure before returning to their arbitrary scrutiny of magazines which were mostly several years old and a steady grumble about 'the system'. On days like this Gemma couldn't blame them, especially as she picked her way carefully through abandoned umbrellas and bags, her smile the only bright thing on a very damp, depressing afternoon.

She side-stepped a child who was promptly walloped soundly for getting in her way. He glared resentfully in Gemma's direction and proceeded to wail loudly for the next half hour. With lungs like that he obviously isn't for the chest clinic, she thought, wincing as the sound followed her in the direction of the desk.

'Good afternoon, Sister. I've been sent over from Casualty to help out.'

Sister Peace's manner was clearly affected by her surroundings. 'And not before time,' she snapped ungraciously. 'I suppose you're all they sent?'

'Yes, I'm afraid so, Sister.' Gemma bit back a depressing feeling that a bad day was suddenly about to become worse.

'I might have known it. It's like asking for charity. It always seems to begin somewhere else. How they expect me to run this department efficiently I don't know, with about half the staff we really need.'

Looking round, Gemma could see an abundance of nurses in varying shades of uniform scurrying intently in all directions, but clearly Sister Peace was not happy. She emerged from behind the desk, waylaying a nervous student.

'And where are you going with that, may I ask?'

The girl stared at the object in her trembling hands. 'To Pathology, Sister. Dr Forbes wants . . .'

'Oh, does he, indeed?' Sister's expression changed slightly. 'Well get a move on then, and don't waste time down there gossiping. I want to see you back in five minutes. These doctors . . .'

Gemma flung a quick look of sympathy in the petrified girl's direction as she fled. Working under Sister Peace, it seemed, was likely to be anything but peaceful.

'You'll have to take the medical clinic.'

Following closely on Sister's heels, skipping a little to keep up, Gemma couldn't help noticing the sudden looks of dismayed anxiety on some of the patients' faces as she was swept past the rows of chairs and into Reception again.

'This lot will be yours.' Sister Peace took a large pile of files from the desk, dropped them into Gemma's hands and allowed a gleam of satisfaction to relax her features. 'There are hundreds. You'll be lucky to finish by six. What time are you due off?'

'Five, Sister.'

'Oh well, it looks as if you'll be a little late then, won't you? I hope you don't have a date. He'll probably get tired of waiting,' she added spitefully.

Gemma deliberately didn't respond, feeling that to do so would only be to invite further antagonism. 'I'm in no hurry, Sister,' she said mildly.

'Good.' The stout figure indicated a door. 'That's the consulting room. Normally I would let you have a student to help but I'm afraid I can't spare one this afternoon so you'll just have to manage as best you can.'

The implication that it was not likely to be a very good best was not lost on Gemma, but she managed to keep smiling. 'I expect I'll cope, Sister.'

The answering look again maliciously seemed to doubt it, and indeed, as she glanced through the mountain of case notes, Gemma felt her own confidence waver until common sense returned. Nursing was nursing, she told herself firmly. The principles were the same wherever she worked and she was not about to let Sister Peace's pettiness upset her.

That resolved, she lifted her chin and marched resolutely into the consulting room, scarcely sparing a glance for the figure who had his back to her as he scrubbed his hands at the wash-basin.

She put the case notes on to the desk, a frown of concentration furrowing her brow as she placed each one in order according to the list of appointments on top, then turned to check that the examination trolley was properly equipped with all the instruments likely to be necessary.

'I'm afraid we don't appear to have a stethoscope, sir,' she addressed the anonymous back without turning. 'I'll pop along to Sister and see if I can get one.'

'Don't worry about it. I'm afraid I'm the culprit.'

The smile faded from her face as Niall Barratt turned and reached for his white coat. She felt the colour drain from her face. 'You!'

'Is something bothering you, Staff Nurse?'

Feeling trapped, she stared at him. 'No . . . no, sir.'

'Good, then perhaps we can get on.' He buttoned the white coat, reached into a pocket and handed her the stethoscope. 'All in order?'

She ground her teeth together and reached for the first of the case notes, slapping it into his hands. 'Yes, of course, sir. I'm afraid it looks like being a heavy list if the crowd out there is anything to go by.'

'In that case, don't you think the sooner we get started, the better?'

The coldness in his voice was almost like a slap in

the face and Gemma felt the resentment wash over her as she stood hesitating. How would she ever understand an enigma like Niall Barratt? A man who could kiss her one day and behave as if he had ice in his veins the next. More to the point, did she want to? It was a bit like Pandora's box. Some things were best left untampered with, and that included her own emotions.

She came too with a start, realising that she had been staring and he was returning the look with a frown of annoyance.

'Well, hadn't you better bring in the first patient? We're going to be here all night otherwise, and while that might suit you, I'm afraid I would find it highly inconvenient.'

Gemma clamped her mouth into a rigid line. No doubt he would, she thought and it occurred to her for the first time, as she turned on her heel and marched quickly out into reception in search of the first patient, that she really knew nothing about him at all as far as his private life was concerned. Not even if there was a woman in his life, though if it was the case he had certainly kept it quiet. She sighed crossly. After all, it was of no interest to her what he did with his life outside the hospital. His manner made it perfectly clear that, as far as he was concerned, their relationship was strictly professional, and that suited her perfectly. All the same, she spent the remainder of the afternoon wondering just who he was in such a hurry to meet.

They worked solidly for the first hour, making what seemed to be very little impression on the list as she brought in one patient after the other, helped them to unfasten clothing, weighed them, removed dressings, whisked back and forth to X-ray or Pathology and generally tried to ensure that everything necessary to enable him to deal smoothly and efficiently with each case was to hand.

By mid-afternoon her head ached. Reception was still moderately full and the windows were steamed up from wet clothing and warm humanity. Without being aware of it, Gemma pressed a hand briefly to her head and thought of the bliss of being able to get off duty and put her feet up.

'Why don't you take a coffee-break?' The words brought her, blushing, out of her reverie and her lips compressed.

'No, thank you, sir. I'm perfectly capable of going without. In fact I'd rather.' She permitted herself a half-smile. 'I'd say they could do with coffee far more than I could.' She nodded in the direction of the hall and was surprised by the tinge of anger in his response.

'In an ideal situation they wouldn't have to put up with conditions like this. But God knows when it will change.' He brushed a hand through his hair and she was suddenly conscious of the lines of weariness around his eyes. 'Oh, I know we have an appointments system, but how can you allocate five minutes to someone you know perfectly well probably isn't going to live another twelve months, or someone who is scared to death of being admitted to hospital again because of the hardship it will cause his family?'

There were some doctors who seemed to manage all too easily, she thought. They seemed to develop an ability to switch off to everything except the patient's immediate physical needs and didn't wish to know what went on behind the details written on the case notes—to the real person. It struck her forcibly that Niall Barratt was an exception. She had been impressed by the way he dealt with each one as an individual, the gentleness and compassion with which he listened.

She kept her voice deliberately light. 'What a pity we can't send round a trolley of tea. I'm sure they'd appreciate it.'

His mouth relaxed slightly. 'Why not hot-buttered toast as well? I'm rather partial to it myself, especially with raspberry jam.'

The sudden and very vivid image of him indulging in anything so remotely human made her blink. Then the image faded.

'So shall we push on then, Staff, and perhaps we can all get home to our . . . various pursuits, whatever they may be.'

It was there again, the note of hostility, and she could think of no justification for it, which only made it hurt all the more. Or perhaps she had imagined it, she told herself. After all, they were both tired. It seemed a long time since lunch and an even longer time until she could escape to the bath and early night she had already promised herself.

The hall did clear gradually. She brought the next patient in, helped her off with mackintosh, woolly cardigan and blouse and busied herself at the trolley as Niall Barratt made his examination. When it was over she helped the woman to dress again and he nodded quietly in her direction, telling her that she was free to go in search of the next patient.

The gynae clinic had finished. ENT were almost on their last and Sister Peace was wearing a smug expression as Gemma appeared, frowning at the names still on her list.

'Not doing too well, are we, Staff? It doesn't usually take quite this long, but then, you're not exactly experienced at Out-patients work, are you?'

Gemma controlled her temper and managed to smile. She couldn't fight Sister Peace's resentment of nurses she considered to be 'outsiders', those who weren't totally dedicated to the idea that Out-patients was the be all and end all of a nursing career.

'I'm afraid not, Sister, but I think I'll just about cope. Not many more, anyway.'

'Yes, well I'll have to leave you to it. I'm off until tomorrow afternoon.'

Probably much to the relief of all her staff, Gemma couldn't help thinking as she watched the stout figure amble away and returned her attention to the two figures still sitting on the rows of chairs. Two? That was odd. All the names bar one on her list were crossed out.

'Mr Grover?'

The man rose wearily and was led into the consulting room.

'Mr Grover, sir. He should be the last but we seem to have acquired an extra one. I'll make some enquiries. There may have been a last-minute appointment.'

'Fine. I shan't need you here.' His gaze drifted over her, suddenly making her aware of the stray wisps of hair escaping from her cap before he turned his attention to the man seated before him. 'Now, Mr Grover. How's this hand of yours? Any problems moving the fingers?'

She walked back into the hall, wishing with slight annoyance that Reception had had the courtesy to tell her there was a last-minute appointment. No doubt she would have to go in search of case notes.

She approached the slumped figure in the chair

and at once felt a slight pang of alarm. Even before she came close enough to ask his name she could smell the alcohol and paused, warily, to look for some kind of assistance, just in case. At least it explained why his name hadn't been on the list. The man had obviously come in out of the cold and was canny enough to know that, in a place like this, with staff and patients constantly coming and going, he could probably get away without being discovered for quite a while.

'Excuse me, but I'm afraid I shall have to ask you to leave.'

He woke, took in the pretty face and struggled to focus more clearly as he grinned. 'Ah, go on, just when I was nice and comfy too. You wouldn't turn me out now, would you? Not a nice little thing like you.'

'I'm afraid you really can't stay here.' He staggered to his feet and Gemma recoiled as whisky fumes hit her full in the face. Her gaze went to Reception. The desk was empty and the door of the consulting room firmly closed. She told herself to stay calm. Drunks were not always violent and so far the man presented no real problem.

'I'm sorry, but you'll have to go. This is a hospital and you really shouldn't be here, you know, unless you need to see a doctor. You don't have an appointment, do you?'

He scratched the stubble on his chin and eyed her speculatively. 'And where is the good doctor then? I don't see him.'

'No.' She swallowed hard as he moved fractionally towards her, lurching against the chairs. 'He's in the consulting room with a patient.'

The man's glance went towards the closed door. 'Is he now? And I suppose you help him, do you?'

He swayed. 'Stand by, like the angel of mercy you are, in case he needs you. That sort of thing.'

She nodded. 'Something like that.' She wished someone would come. The man showed no sign of wanting to leave and she stared as he took a half-bottle of whisky from his pocket and drank from it, reeling slightly.

'Lucky man, that old doctor, having a nice girl like you to watch out for him. Wouldn't mind a job like that myself. Pretty girl like you shouldn't be in a place like this though.'

She couldn't help agreeing with him at this precise moment. He reached out a hand and she flinched as he touched her hair. He laughed and before she knew what was happening he had whisked the cap roughly away, pulling the pins so that her hair fell from its neatly coiled bun to her shoulders. She reached for it, protesting, only to have her hand gripped in a sweaty palm as the man pulled her closer.

'Come on now, be nice. Let's be friends.'

She cried out as his face rasped against hers and she felt her stomach tighten as he breathed whisky over her. 'Let me go, please.'

He chuckled and swayed, but didn't release his grasp. She twisted to look helplessly at the consulting room door, wondering if anyone would hear, were she to scream, but the intention died as the man's mouth was suddenly pressed over hers, bringing waves of nausea as she struggled in sheer panic. Instinct made her jam her foot down hard on his shin. It did no real damage, her shoes were too soft, but at least it was sufficient to make him release his hold and gave her a few seconds advantage. She thrust herself away, but not before he had snatched at her dress and she heard it tear across the shoulder before he caught her again, this time in a grip which drew a frightened scream of pain from her. Why didn't anyone see what was happening?

She slipped as the man lunged at her again, her foot grating painfully against one of the chairs as it fell. Her eyes closed, waiting, dreading, but somehow he didn't reach her. When she opened them again Niall was there, standing quietly beside her, reaching down to help her up as he looked at the man.

She marvelled as he said calmly, in a voice which seemed to belie the ice-cold anger she glimpsed in his eyes, 'I think you've done enough damage, don't you? I suggest you get out now, before I have to call the police. Find somewhere else to sleep it off, there's a good chap.'

Through a mist of tears and pain from her bruised ankle, Gemma saw the man hesitate and felt Niall Barratt's hand tighten as he bent to help her to her feet. She was shaking so violently that she leaned against him for a moment.

'I don't suppose you could spare a wee something for a dram?' The drunk wiped a hand across his mouth, saw the look in the senior registrar's eyes and nodded unsteadily. 'Aye, I suppose not.' Grinning, he lurched away and Gemma released her breath slowly.

'Are you all right?'

If only she could stop shaking. 'Yes, of course.'

His frowning gaze moved disconcertingly over her and her hand went involuntarily to the tear in her dress as she realised with a gasp of horror that it was worse than she had imagined. She dragged the edges together to cover what seemed like a vast expanse of sun-tanned shoulder and breast. Her face felt suddenly hot as she looked up, wishing him, and the cool touch of his hands on her naked shoulders, at least a million miles away. For one crazy moment his face swam closer and she could feel his breath on her skin.

She closed her eyes, wishing her heart would stop reacting so crazily, and then he jerked away.

'I'd better go and make sure he's really off the premises or God knows what mischief he'll get up to.' His gaze flickered to her dress. 'Don't worry, it's only the seam. I'm sure you'll be able to repair it without too much trouble, so no harm's done.'

She was still trembling as he walked away, but suddenly it was anger at herself that caused it. No harm done? She wished she could say it with as much conviction, but the memory of his hands on her naked skin was still far too vivid as she turned and fled to the blissful privacy of the now empty consulting room where she closed the door and promptly burst into tears.

By the time he returned, several minutes later, she had managed to recover at least some of her composure. She had secured her dress with safety-pins and was inspecting her face in the mirror when he came to stand behind her.

'Mm, that's quite a nasty scratch you've got there. Better let me put something on it.'

She turned quickly. 'There's really no need. I've bathed it.' It wasn't strictly true. She had dashed cold water on her cheeks in an attempt to cool them, an exercise which, she realised with a certain amount of chagrin, had been somewhat super-fluous because there was nothing but professional interest in his eyes as he approached her. And why had she expected anything else, she asked herself crossly. He was, after all, a doctor—quite accustomed to seeing patients in various stages of undress all day and every day.

'All the same, I think I'll take a look. We don't want to take any chances, do we? Just sit down. It won't take a minute.' He nodded towards the chair and she sat, despising herself all over again as he came to her and began gently swabbing the scratch. It wasn't fair, she thought. It wasn't fair . . . Then his fingers went to her shoulder and before she knew what was happening he had deftly removed the safety pins and was examining her.

She jerked away defensively. 'There's really no need, Doctor. I'm perfectly all right.'

His brows furrowed. 'As it happens, you have quite a nasty bruise and if you'll just sit still long enough I'll deal with it.'

She felt the tears of frustration stinging at her lashes. 'I'm sure it will be perfectly all right by morning.'

'On the contrary, by morning it will probably be quite painful and you're not likely to be much use at your job if you can't move properly, are you?'

There was quiet sarcasm in his gaze and she sat, biting her lip, wishing he would hurry and get it over with. His white coat brushed against her as he worked and she found herself staring at his shirt and caught a faint whiff of aftershave. She closed her eyes, forcing herself to think of a long, hot bath in which she could soak away all the humiliation and the aches. Anything rather than the sensations his touch was sending through her.

'There we are.' Almost as if he was laughing at her, he refastened the safety-pins 'Modesty restored. You still look a little flushed though.'

She got to her feet quickly and only just managed not to wince as her bruised ankle made contact with the floor. 'It's just a bit of a headache, that's all. I'll take some aspirin when I get home.'

He removed the basin of antiseptic and was washing his hands as she realised with a sense of shock that she hadn't returned the case notes to Reception. She began to gather them up.

'Leave those,' he flung over his shoulder sharply. 'I'll see to them later.'

'But I . . . I have to return them.'

'I have to come back anyway. I've some notes to write up. Get your coat. I'll be with you in two minutes and take you home.'

Feeling trapped, she stood shaking. 'There's no need. I can drive myself quite easily.'

'I don't think so.' There was mild annoyance in his voice as he looked at her now. 'Allow me to know best in this instance. You're still in a state of shock and that shoulder is going to give you more trouble than you realise right now. It will be safer for me to drive you and it won't be any inconvenience—provided, of course, we don't stand here for the next half-hour arguing about it.'

Gemma bit back a feeling of angry frustration. What she wanted more than anything was to escape, to put as much distance as possible between herself and the awful embarrassment of what had happened. But to her chagrin she had to admit that he was right when she climbed into his car minutes later, trying not to wince as she jarred her shoulder. She wasn't capable of driving properly.

'Will you be able to get in in the morning without your own car?'

She was glad he couldn't see her as she nodded in the darkness. The cut on her cheek was sore and her entire body ached. 'I can catch a bus. They run quite close to the flat.'

He was silent and she felt the hot tears ooze up between her lashes as she turned to stare resolutely out of the window, seeing nothing. She gulped with misery and jumped as he said, quietly,

'For heaven's sake, have a good cry and get it over with. You're taking it all much too seriously, you know.'

She swallowed hard, fumbled for a hanky and took the one he proffered. What did he know about it anyway? She wasn't crying for anything in particular, just . . . everything in general. Suddenly everything seemed to be going wrong and he wasn't helping matters. Life had been quietly uncomplicated before he had come along, interfering, self-opinionated . . . A tear ran down her cheek. 'I'm just tired, that's all.'

He turned to glance at her, then back at the road. 'You've still got to acquire a tough skin. It helps, you know. If you wear your heart on your sleeve you're bound to get hurt. Nursing isn't the image you've dreamed up for yourself, Gemma. It's hard and tough and if you can't handle it you'd be better off doing something else.'

She couldn't believe he was saying the cruel words. 'Are you trying to tell me I'm no good at my job?' She sat rigidly in the seat, feeling deflated and miserable.

His gaze flickered briefly in her direction again as the car drew to a halt outside the flat, but neither of them made any attempt to move. She felt too tired, too bruised both physically and mentally.

'I'm saying that hysterics don't help.'

'Hysterics?' she screeched. 'I am *not* hysterical! I have never in my life been hysterical.'

'No?' In the light of the street lamp she saw his dark brow wing upwards.

'Well just how do you expect me to react to being manhandled by a drunk? Am I supposed to throw myself at every male patient who makes a pass at me, or worse?' She shivered.

'That's not what I'm saying at all, and you know it.' He had turned to face her, his arm along the seat so that it brushed against her hair. In the confinement of the car his nearness seemed to be having an even stranger effect upon her nerves and she flinched as his fingers brushed unexpectedly against her cheek.

'Just what is it you're afraid of, Gemma?'

'I'm not afraid.' Her laugh sounded shrill.

'No?'

She closed her eyes and clenched her teeth together as he moved closer and with slow deliberation took her in his arms. Weakly she willed him not to, but if he sensed her resistance he ignored it. His finger traced the line of her cheek and she felt her breath falter as his mouth came closer, tantalising her with its warm desirability so that her own lips parted in a soft groan and the sensuous mouth closed over hers.

She had been fooling herself, she knew it instantly, in thinking she could remain indifferent. The kiss seemed to plunder her senses, drawing responses from her she would have held back, betraying her into feelings she had told herself she would never experience again. Desire coursed through her veins and she knew she was shaking but didn't want it to end. He moaned softly against her hair, releasing her mouth for a second, then claiming it again, more brutally this time, as if sensing her reluctance slipping away. Gemma felt a tide of longing surge through her.

Don't let it stop, some inner voice pleaded.

Don't ever let it stop. Her lips parted hungrily and she felt the instant response in him, caught the faint aroma of aftershave as she lay against the masculine hardness of his chest.

'I love you.' His voice was hoarse. 'You must know I do.'

She didn't want to fight the sense of urgency which was engulfing her. It had been so long since her body had felt such need, been allowed to feel. Too long since Bill had held her in his arms. Would he have expected her to live her life with mere memories? Was that what she wanted? She had only to let go . . .

A sob suddenly caught in her throat and she stiffened in his arms. What was she doing? She tried to drag herself away, felt his hands tighten.

'Gemma.'

'No . . . no, please, don't.' She couldn't go through it all again, all the loving and then the pain, the inevitable, cruel pain.

'Gemma, what is it?' She saw the turmoil in his eyes as she fought blindly, panicking as she sensed how little it would take to make her surrender. If he kissed her again . . . Her head jerked away.

'I won't ever be hurt again. I've been through it and I don't intend to let it happen, not a second time.'

He released her abruptly, his face white and grim as he stared at her. 'Some day it may just happen and you won't be able to fight it.'

She shook her head, turned away, still trembling as she pressed a hand to her mouth. 'I won't let it.' The words were whispered but she thought in sudden terror, it's happening already. It's too late. I'm already in love with him.

She felt him draw away from her and was glad of

the darkness which hid the tears coursing down her cheeks.

'No one can run away for ever, Gemma.'

She couldn't speak, daren't look at him, or she knew she would be in his arms and lost for ever.

'You think you've been hurt.' His voice was grim. 'But you don't know what life or pain is really all about. You're still a child, Gemma, still naive.'

The words caught her on the raw. How dare he make judgments? 'And I suppose you do?' She flung at him.

'I think so.' His voice was quiet. 'And if you're really so sure you're right, why not put it to the test?'

She frowned. 'I don't know what you mean.'

He reached for the ignition key, not looking at her. 'It's simple. If you want to see what real tragedy is, why don't you work in the Trauma Unit for a while. They do know what it's all about. The difference is, they still have the guts to fight.'

She rounded on him, furiously. 'And you're saying I haven't?'

He looked at her. 'You've given up, taken the easy way out.'

'That isn't true.'

'Oh, but I think it is. You got hurt once, so instead of facing up to life and getting on with it, you've decided to play it safe by cutting yourself off from reality and any risk. Well that's fine, until you start playing with other people's feelings. They do have them too you know.' He thrust the door open. 'At least I found out where I stand. I certainly won't make the same mistake again, you can count on that.'

He held the door open and she climbed out

feeling numb. For a second they faced each other, inches apart. She had only to reach out . . .

'Goodnight, Gemma. Sweet dreams. They're far safer than the real thing.'

She caught the faint bitterness in the words and then he was gone, leaving her to stare after the car, feeling as if part of her life had gone with him.

# CHAPTER TWELVE

MISS DRAKE's features wore a harassed look. 'As it happens we could certainly use you on the new unit. The planners seem to have the idea that once their part is done, ours automatically follows. If only they realised it isn't quite that simple. Staffing a new unit, and particularly one of this type, is never easy.' A tapping at the door was ignored as she reached for the button which would flick on the engaged sign. Her gaze returned to Gemma. 'May I ask why you wish to be transferred to the trauma unit?'

Gemma had been steeling herself for the inevitable question. 'I think I could be useful there.'

'Ah.' A weary smile briefly lit Miss Drake's face. 'I seem to have heard that phrase a great deal during the past few weeks. Unfortunately it doesn't tell me much and I have to point out that the trauma unit requires a particular kind of temperament and dedication from the nurses who work there.'

'Yes, Miss Drake, I realise that.' Gemma felt her pulses race at the word. 'I feel I could do the work. I would like to,' she added almost with a hint of defiance. 'I enjoyed my brief spell on theatre and Intensive Care during training.'

'Yes, so I gather. Sister's reports on your work were very good.' The grey eyes were suddenly levelled shrewdly in Gemma's direction. 'You do appreciate fully what would be involved? The patients who come to the unit are going to be those most desperately in need of immediate care, whose

143

lives will, quite literally, be in your hands and those of the rest of the team. These will be the most severely injured or sick patients.'

'Yes, I do.'

The DNS nodded. 'This unit is something of an innovation for us. A great many eyes will be watching to see that we, and it, justify its existence.'

'But how can it not?' Gemma protested unthinkingly.

Miss Drake smiled sadly. 'I share your sentiments, Staff Nurse. Unfortunately, like it or not, finance is a major consideration. The unit cost a great deal and we only got it because the arguments used were forceful enough to prove a need. But now it's up to us to prove ourselves capable of fulfilling that need.' Long fingers tapped against the desk. 'There are always areas of nursing which seem to have to suffer for someone else's gain. It isn't fair, but then life seldom is.'

Gemma agreed in silence. Life was very unfair. If it weren't, there wouldn't be men like Niall Barratt. She dragged her attention back quickly.

'You were assigned to Accident and Emergency on a temporary basis.'

'Yes, Miss Drake.'

'Not a policy I generally approve. It causes too much disruption for staff as well as patients, but at least in A and E continuity of care is hardly the same factor.'

Gemma took a deep breath. 'That's the main reason I didn't enjoy it as much as being on the wards. I like to get to know my patients.' She looked intently at the older woman and saw an answering frown.

'Getting to know them is one thing. Getting involved is quite another. I assume you appreciate there is a subtle difference?'

'I . . . I think so.' Gemma felt a moment of inner panic. It was easy to say, but how could she be sure? How would she cope with someone critically ill, perhaps disfigured for life, or someone who would never walk again? How did one not become involved? Bill had said once that she took everything too much to heart. She had laughed the argument aside until now. Perhaps she *was* making a mistake. Then Niall Barratt's words hit her with a kind of savage force. *You don't know what real life and tragedy is all about.* Well, she would prove him wrong. She lifted her face to Miss Drake's.

'I'm sure I do appreciate the difference, and I believe I could cope.'

She held her breath in silence, unaware that the older woman was shrewdly watching and assessing the variety of emotions which flickered over the staff nurse's pale face. There was a kind of intensity about them which made the DNS hesitate. She had seen the look before, that kind of determination, and wondered why it left her feeling vaguely uneasy in this instance. She frowned and made an instant decision.

'We do still need staff for the unit. Some have been recruited as a matter of course, because of their seniority and past experience. In your case . . .' She scanned the file in front of her. 'We've had excellent reports throughout your training and your examination results certainly seem to justify allowing you to go to the unit.'

Gemma gave a tremulous gasp of relief. 'Oh, thank you.'

'Don't thank me.' Miss Drake rose to her feet. 'In a month's time you may be sitting there begging me to remove you to a ward. You may as well know

now that I shall be very displeased if that happens.'

'Oh, it won't..I'm sure it won't.' Gemma was on her feet too, now.

'Yes, well, report to the unit first thing on Monday morning. Sister Pepper will be on duty, taking over from Sister Wang on nights. I suggest you arrive early and get to know both.'

'Yes, Miss Drake. I will.'

Gemma left the office and went back to A and E in a daze. Now that the move was actually made she felt an odd mixture of relief and panic. She drew a deep, steadying breath and told herself firmly that she was being ridiculous.

Gemma reached for a pile of case notes and found herself battling with a sudden wave of depression at the thought that what she had always wanted suddenly didn't seem to hold the same importance any more. She closed her eyes against the ruthless image of a stern jaw and a mouth which had the power to rob her of every shred of resistance unless she was very, very careful, and she was determined it wouldn't happen. She had something else to fill her life now, and it wouldn't leave room for interruptions, least of all Niall Barratt.

It was like stepping into a new world, Gemma thought, entering the portals of the trauma unit for the first time and trying desperately to banish the feeling that she was a raw probationer all over again. The similarities were too strong to be ignored and she almost found herself tiptoeing as she entered the light, spacious area of reception.

'I'm to report to Sister Pepper.'

The girl at the desk smiled. 'Through those doors, along the corridor. You'll see the office on your right.'

'Thanks.'

Gemma found herself trying to relate the months of builder's rubble and scaffolding to the miracle of the finished building without much success as she walked along the corridor and tapped at the door. A voice beckoned her in and she entered to see three figures, all wearing the navy uniform of sisters. Trusting to luck, she addressed the one at the desk.

'Good morning, Sister Pepper. I'm Staff Nurse Lawson. I was told to report for duty.'

'I'm Sister Pepper.' A tall, auburn-haired figure smiled as she closed the filing cabinet. 'You're nice and early.'

'I thought it might be a good idea to get my bearings a little first.' Gemma felt herself begin to relax.

'Good idea. I gather you're over from A and E.'

'Yes, that's right. Although it was only temporary. As a matter of fact I was only made up to Staff recently.'

'Oh well, we all have to start somewhere. You're not nervous are you?'

'Well . . . a little.'

A ripple of sympathetic laughter made her look more closely at the girl seated at the desk as Sister Wang eased herself wearily out of the chair.

'Here, Pepper. You'd better take over before I fall asleep.' She had a beautiful dark-haired, dark-eyed grace which looked particularly stunning in uniform, Gemma noticed with a twinge of envy. 'I hope you know what you're letting yourself in for.' She yawned. 'I shan't be sorry to get to my bed. The report's going to take a while to get through. We had quite a hectic night. Not that that's at all unusual here.' Her glance went to Gemma. 'Most of our admissions are road traffic accidents and the majority seem to come in late at night.'

'Why don't you find yourself a perch?' Jan Pepper nodded towards a chair and reached for the book. 'We're just about to go through the report anyway, so you'll get a rough idea of the picture. Then I'll get Sister Travers to show you around. Don't worry, there's not really a great deal to see.' The reassurance came as the door opened and several other members of the on-coming day staff began to drift in.

Gemma began to wonder if she would ever be able to remember all the names, but within minutes her attention was absorbed as the general babble of laughter and early-morning chatter faded and the formal business of the report began. It soon became obvious that the trauma unit was going to be like nothing she had ever experienced before and she felt the nervous churning in her stomach as she listened and watched the rapt faces around her.

Fifteen minutes later, feeling decidedly dazed, she filed out into the corridor and watched the nurses disperse to their various duties.

'Best of luck.' Sister Wang waved and disappeared through the swing doors and Jan Pepper girded her loins for the day ahead with brisk but smiling efficiency.

'Don't look so nervous! It's really not so bad once you get used to the routine. When you get down to the nitty-gritty it's all nursing. The important thing to remember is that here we work as a team. We work quickly and quietly. The patient's life literally depends upon each of us doing our job to the best of our ability and being able to work together.'

She looked at her watch. 'I'd better go and catch

that damned Irish man before he disappears again. Can I leave you to show her the ropes?'

Elaine Travers grinned. 'Will do.'

Gemma watched the departing figure with some trepidation. 'Damned Irishman?'

'Oh, she means our Mr O'Hara. Ophthalmic registrar. The joke here is that if you blink you miss him. Not that you can. He has red hair too.' She lowered her voice. 'He and Sister don't hit it off too well—on the surface, that is. Deep down I suspect they have a sort of love-hate relationship, but you can never tie the wretched man down long enough to find out.' They walked along the corridor together, Gemma trying to absorb her surroundings as well as what was being said. 'Don't get me wrong. He's brilliant at his job. He wouldn't be on the unit otherwise.' They turned into a side corridor and went through another door.

'This is where the emergency admissions come in and the preliminary examination is made. Good morning, Nurses.' Several pairs of eyes were turned briefly in their direction and a chorus of greetings. A third year nurse wearing a white dress with red braid trimmings looked up from the trolley she was checking.

'Morning, Sister. Morning, Staff.' She smiled shyly in Gemma's direction. 'I understand Mr Stone wants to see Gregory Tyler in theatre again this morning.'

'Yes, that's right, but not until Mr O'Hara has finished the corneal repair. Mr Stone wants to take over and do a manipulation on the fractured femur and perhaps cut down the plaster a little. It means the patient only has to be anaesthetised and taken up to theatre once. Is everything ready?'

'Yes, Sister. The pre-med was given half an hour

ago. He should be going into theatre any time now.'

'Fine. Well, Staff Nurse Lawson will be joining us later, once I've shown her the ropes. Let's hope she doesn't have too dramatic an initiation.'

'That's a bit like wishing an actor good luck.' Nurse Parker gave Gemma a sympathetic grin. 'Still, you never know. Miracles do happen, or so they say.'

The rest of the morning passed in something of a dream. By the time she was sent for lunch, Gemma's head was spinning with information, most of which she was sure she would never remember, and she ate her meal without even being aware of what it was. *We work as a team.* Sister's words came back to her as she chewed solidly at a Yorkshire pudding. *You'll notice we have what might seem a disproportionate quota of staff.* She had indeed noticed several sisters, not all wearing the same uniform. Some wore the traditional navy, some wore white dresses with navy trim, Junior Sisters, and some wore distinctive red dresses beneath the white apron, Unit Theatre Sisters.

She was just frowning into her second cup of coffee when a figure slipped into the seat opposite.

'You don't mind if I join you, do you?' Sue Foster put her own cup down. 'You seem to be in a world of your own. I've been waving frantically at you for the past five minutes.'

'Sorry. I started on the trauma unit today and my head is reeling. Honestly, Sue, I'm wondering if I'm up to it.'

'What, already?' Sue spooned sugar into her cup. 'For heaven's sake, give it a chance. You haven't been there long enough to get your apron dirty yet! Besides, I thought this was what you wanted. Some real nursing.'

'Yes, it is. Only . . . well—oh, I don't know, it's so scary, knowing that so much depends on what you do, making absolutely the right move.'

'My dear girl, I was under the impression that that's what nursing is all about. Taking responsibility. You'll be all right. It's just first day nerves.'

'I hope you're right.' Gemma sipped at her coffee and watched the queues gathering. 'What brings you here, anyway? It's becoming rather a habit, isn't it?'

'Oh I've been up to see Miss Drake again, actually.'

'What, about your transfer to days? Any luck?'

Sue shrugged. 'I'm not sure you could call it that.' She traced a ring of spilt coffee with the spoon.

'How do you mean?'

'She offered me days on Rosemary Ward, in a couple of months' time. I gather Mitford is retiring.'

'But that's marvellous—that you've been offered it, I mean.'

'Yes.' Sue suddenly seemed to be avoiding her eyes. 'Unfortunately it isn't quite that simple.'

'But why? I thought it was exactly what you wanted? I know it's not for a few weeks, but surely you can hang on.'

'Yes. It's not that that's the problem.' Sue pushed her cup away and looked at her watch. 'Look, there isn't time to explain it now. Could I possibly come over to your place and have a chat . . . tonight, say?'

'Well yes, of course you can. You know you don't need to ask. But what's wrong?'

Sue got to her feet. 'It's a bit complicated. I'll tell you then. I have to go now.'

'You haven't even finished your coffee.'

'That's all right, I didn't really want it anyway.'
She hoisted the straps of her bag on to her shoulder.
'I'll see you tonight then, okay?'

'Yes, fine, but why don't you wait and catch
Dick? He sometimes comes in.'

'No.' Her gaze darted to the door. 'Well . . . I
would but I've got some shopping to do and I
haven't really had much sleep since I came off duty
this morning, so I ought to catch up.'

Gemma watched her walk away and rose slowly
to her own feet. It was only then that she realised
she wouldn't be finished until six and that she was
already feeling exhausted.

Sister greeted her arrival back on the unit with a
look of relief as she hurried towards her. 'Oh, Staff,
we have an emergency on its way in. Road traffic
accident.' She gave a resigned smile. 'Two involved. Police are escorting the ambulance in. We
never quite know what to expect so we have to be
prepared for anything.'

Gemma felt the quick surge of adrenalin. 'Yes,
Sister. Where would you like me to start?'

'Warn theatre, will you? Number one is in use so
two and three will have to stand by. Then check
that everything is ready for the preliminary examinations. Oxygen, gloves. All the usual.'

Sister hurried away and Gemma found herself
responding automatically as she walked quickly
into the admission area and began to satisfy herself
that all was in readiness. Almost without being
aware of it she became part of the team, feeling the
nervousness slip away as training took over, and by
the time the ambulance had drawn up and the first
stretcher was being wheeled in, the tempo of the
unit had already undergone a subtle change as

everyone swung quietly into action.

The first patient was put gently on to the table. Gemma scarcely had time to take in the bloody mass that had once been a face before her actions became instinctive and she worked without thinking. All other emotions had to be pushed aside. There was no time for pity or anger as she swabbed away blood, standing aside, fresh swabs at the ready, as the medical team took over. She found herself treated to a brief smile as Lliam O'Hara, red hair concealed beneath a cap, bent over the unconscious man, his face tense with concentration as he worked to save the badly gashed eyes. Beside him the neurological registrar examined a head wound and throughout, the routine checks went on.

'Blood pressure is falling, sir. The heart rate is fast.'

'He's going to need a transfusion. He's lost a lot of blood.'

'Let's get him to theatre. Get John Spencer in, will you, Sister? He'll have to see to that thigh. There's a bad fracture. It will probably need pinning.'

There was no let-up. It was like a wave, slowly gathering momentum, carrying them towards the moment when the man was wheeled into theatre, then washing quietly back as they cleared and prepared, ready for the next admission.

As if she was coming out of a dream, Gemma became aware of Sister Pepper at her side saying, 'Well done, Staff. That wasn't so bad, was it? You can go off as soon as you've cleared. I'll see you in the morning.'

It wasn't until she got outside and the cold air hit her as she walked across the car park, that Gemma realised she had survived her first day on the trauma unit and it hadn't been quite as bad as she had expected.

Back at the flat she heated tomato soup and carried it through to the sitting-room to sit in front of the gas fire. She stared into the flames reflectively. One way and another it had been quite a day. She hadn't seen Niall Barratt and she had survived that too!

The door bell rang and she went to let Sue in.

'Sorry, I forgot you'd probably be having your supper.'

'I'm not.' Gemma grimaced at the cold remnants. 'I've gone off it. I don't think it was a wise choice. Anyway, let me take your coat and we'll have some coffee. It's all ready.'

She returned from the kitchen to find Sue huddled in front of the fire, surreptitiously hiding a hanky in her pocket. The fact that her reddened eyes might betray its purpose seemed to have escaped her as she began to talk far too brightly and with a note of desperation which made Gemma realise that her friend needed far more than a mere chat.

She let it go for a while, answering questions, knowing that her answers weren't even being registered. Then she put her cup down and said quietly, 'Why not just tell me what's wrong? I'd like to help, you know—if I can.'

Sue sighed lethargically and fumbled for a cigarette. She lit it nervously. 'I'm sorry. I suppose I've been babbling like an idiot.'

'Just a bit.' Gemma smiled. 'Look, if you want to talk about it I'm happy to listen. Or do you just want to go on pretending nothing is wrong?' She put her cup down. 'It won't be easy. I've known you far too long. It's Dick, isn't it?'

She watched as Sue inhaled deeply and clasped her hands shakily together. 'Not exactly. Well, I suppose it is in a way.'

'But I thought that was all sorting itself out? At least now you can tell him about the transfer to days. That should please him.'

'No, I don't think it will. As a matter of fact there's a bit of a problem about the job because I can't take it.'

Gemma sank on to the arm of the settee. 'But why? I don't understand. I thought it was all settled.'

Sue laughed wryly. 'Yes, so did I. The trouble is, it's not quite that easy after all. You see, I'm pregnant.'

Shock widened Gemma's eyes. On reflection she was to wonder why she hadn't suspected it before, but now she laughed. 'Well that's marvellous!'

'Is it?' The cigarette was ground out as Sue got to her feet and began to pace agitatedly.

'Well surely it is? I mean, I know it's perhaps not quite how you planned it . . .'

There was a short, explosive laugh. 'You can say that again!'

'But a baby is a baby. You don't seriously imagine Dick is going to mind? He's as crazy about children as you are.'

'You don't have to tell me that. It's really been the cause of the trouble all along. We both want them.'

'Then I can't believe the fact that it's happened sooner instead of later is really going to make any difference.' Gemma sat down and took Sue's shaking hand in her own. 'These things have a way of working out.'

'I don't see how in this case.' She dragged her

hand away. 'Oh God, what am I going to do?'

'You're going to tell Dick of course.' Gemma had to force the lightness into her voice as she watched her friend's rigid back. 'And he's going to be absolutely over the moon. Believe me, he will.'

Sue spun to face her. 'How can you say that? Don't you see? Nothing has changed, except for the worse. God knows I could perhaps go on working for a while if no one finds out, but can you imagine how long that will be? And then what?' Her eyes glistened with tears. 'There's no way we'll be able to keep the flat and we can't afford the house. It would have been a struggle if I'd kept working but now . . .' She turned away, smothering a sob.

'I take it you haven't actually told Dick yet?'

'No. And I don't intend to.'

Shock held Gemma frozen for a moment. 'But you must! He has a right to know and . . . it will bring you closer together.'

'I don't know that it will.' Sue's response was muffled and Gemma stirred uneasily.

'How can you say that? Surely a baby is something you both have a right to? You could work something out.'

'Like what? I've driven myself nearly crazy trying to come up with answers. There isn't one. I've even spoken to the landlord but it's no use. Even if he agreed, there isn't room at the flat.' She brushed a hand across her eyes. 'I know you're going to hate me for saying it, but I think it might be better if I didn't have this baby.'

Gemma couldn't stifle the soft gasp of disbelief. 'You're not serious? You haven't really thought about what you're saying!'

There was a moment's silence. 'I've thought of nothing else.'

'How long have you known?'

'Since that day I saw you in Casualty. I'd been to the clinic. They confirmed it, although I'd guessed anyway. I suppose I just didn't want to accept it. You know, pretend it's not really happening and it will all go away.' Her mouth compressed. 'But it's not like that, is it?' She looked at Gemma. 'I hate to ask, but would you mind if I stayed again for a while, just long enough to try and think things out?'

'Yes . . . of course you can. If you're sure that's what you want.'

'I'm not sure about anything. That's why I need time.'

'Well I'll make up the spare bed. It's yours for as long as you need it, but what about Dick?'

'I don't know.'

'He's going to want to know where you are.'

'I shouldn't think that's likely. He's away at a conference for a few days anyway. Besides, I'm not at all sure I want to go through another whole series of arguments or, come to that, even if he is interested enough to want to.'

'Not interested? What on earth makes you think otherwise?'

'Oh, I don't know. Several things.'

'Well, like what? Sue, what are you trying to say? Dick is as crazy about you as you are about him. If only the pair of you would get together again and give yourselves time to find out!'

Sue gave a hard little laugh. 'I'd like to think you were right. Unfortunately I have reason to suppose he's consoling himself perfectly happily elsewhere.'

'No!' The gasp of incredulity was wrung from Gemma. 'I don't believe it.'

'That's what I thought at first but . . . Well you

know what the grape-vine is. They say he's seeing someone else.'

'Oh, rubbish! Surely you don't take any notice of that sort of malicious gossip?'

'Don't you?' The challenge came in a look of acute misery.

'No, of course not. You can't honestly believe a fraction of what is said. You know how things get distorted.'

'I thought I did.' Sue's eyes hardened. 'Trouble is, it's never been about Dick before. In any case, he certainly hasn't been at the flat. I know because I've rung several times when he should be there.'

Gemma groaned inwardly. 'That doesn't necessarily mean what you think it means. There could be all sorts of reasons!'

She tried to rack her brains for something she may have missed, but there had been no indication of anything between Dick Foster and another member of staff. Not that her mind had been particularly occupied with anyone else's problems of late, she had to admit.

'Look, I'm sure you're wrong. It just wouldn't be Dick.' Gemma saw from the look on Sue's face that she was fighting a losing battle, for the present anyway. They were both tired. She looked at her watch. 'Why don't we both get some sleep? We might see things more clearly tomorrow.' She headed for the door. 'Dick wouldn't, you know, but the only way you're going to find out, convince yourself, is if you get together and talk.'

Sue nodded. 'You're right. I just don't think I can face it yet though. I'm not even sure I want to know . . .'

She turned away and Gemma fought a feeling of exasperation as she went to make up the bed and

later, after a bath, eventually climbed into her own.
As it happened, in spite of feeling exhausted, she
lay awake for hours. A vision of Niall Barratt
drifted into her mind and she turned over, thump-
ing her pillows as she tried to shut it out.

# CHAPTER THIRTEEN

WITHIN A week it was as if she had always worked on the unit. It had happened surprisingly quickly, Gemma reflected, placing an endotrachial tube on the trolley and checking the supply of sterile dressings. The fact that she scarcely had time to think was a bonus. It was a relief to be able to return to the flat at night too tired to do anything more than bath, eat and fall into bed. She scarcely saw anything of Sue, who came and went like a pale shadow.

Gemma looked up as Lliam O'Hara sauntered into the treatment room and laid a casual hand around her waist. 'And how are you this morning, my little darling?'

'Very well, thank you, sir. And how are you?'

'All the better for a glimpse of those amazingly sexy legs,' he grinned, and made a playful bite at her neck which she managed, smilingly but firmly, to avoid—just as Sister Pepper came in, casting a jaundiced eye in his direction.

'And what exactly are you doing here, disturbing my nurses, Mr O'Hara?' She exchanged an understanding glance with Gemma who had scampered to safety on the other side of the trolley. 'Have you nothing better to do? If not, I'm sure we could find you something, don't you think so, Staff?'

'Yes, I'm sure we could, Sister.' Gemma liked the young Irish registrar, but it hadn't taken long to discover that, beneath the white coat, there was a wolf who flirted outrageously with every nurse on the unit. 'There's the soiled linen still to be sorted.'

'There we are then, Mr O'Hara. I'm sure you'd like to make yourself useful and take some of the workload from my very busy nurses.'

'Sure and you're a hard woman, Sister darling.' Gemma stifled a giggle as he grasped Sister in a mischievous embrace. 'I'll have you know I'm here on perfectly honest and legitimate business.'

'Monkey business, I don't doubt, Mr O'Hara.' She struggled free and eased her dress back to its customary neatness.

'With you, Sister darling, any time.'

'*Mr O'Hara*, unless you get out of my sight this instant I shall be obliged to make life very difficult for you—very difficult indeed.'

The red head was cocked to one side. 'Now you don't mean that, my angel. Sure, isn't life quite difficult enough as it is, me having to restrain this powerful urge I have to kiss your blushing cheeks?'

Gemma turned away, pretending to be engrossed in her work, but she heard the tiny, strangled cry of exasperation in Sister's throat as she advanced menacingly towards him.

'*Out*, Mr O'Hara.'

He reached the door before her, chuckling unrepentantly. 'I'm going, Sister, since my presence rouses such a wild passion in that lovely breast.'

The door swung to a close and Jan Pepper stood, breathing hard—but not, Gemma noticed, without a very attractive blush on her face.

'That man. I swear one day I'll . . .'

The door swung open again. 'Now, now, Sister, you know it's fighting hard y'are to keep your hands off me.'

There was a scream of muffled fury as he kissed her soundly and disappeared, laughing, before she

could regain her breath. To Gemma it seemed that
Sister hadn't struggled very hard, but she managed
to keep a straight face as the slim figure drew
herself up, readjusted her frilled cap and protested
vehemently, 'That man is a menace!'

'Yes, Sister.' Gemma applied herself diligently
to an instrument count for the second time.

'I shall be in my office if anyone needs me.'

'Yes, Sister.' It wasn't until the door had closed
that she realised she still had no idea what either of
them had wanted.

She was just about to go to lunch when the
mugging victim was brought in. The stretcher was
wheeled in, Senior Staff Nurse Johnson keeping
the oxygen mask firmly in place over the patient's
nose and mouth as the porters manoeuvred the
trolley deftly through the doors and into the treatment room.

'Can you stay please, Staff? Here, help get him
on to the bed. Fine, ease him over a little. Right.'
The trolley was whisked away.

Sister Travers appeared, took one look at the
man's erratic breathing and rapped, 'Quickly, he's
going to arrest.'

Within seconds it seemed the room was full of
people, all working with a kind of quiet, controlled
desperation to save the man's life. Gemma guessed
he must be about seventy, but it was difficult to tell
as the features took on the blue look of someone
whose heart had ceased to beat. John Sinclair, the
senior registrar, had come in quietly to take control, but it was still several tense minutes before the
quiet, laboured breathing began again and the air
of tension which had gradually built up began to
relax.

'What happened?'

'A mugging, as far as we can tell.' Sister supplied the information as she began swabbing blood from the man's head. 'They made a pretty mess of him too.' She moved aside and John Sinclair bent closer to make an examination.

'There are at least three broken ribs.' He straightened up grimly and went on to the large gash across the man's cheek-bone. Gemma swabbed the area quickly. Part of the bone was visible and she had to contain a feeling of fury that any human being could inflict such injury on another. 'We're going to have to get him straight into theatre. That facial injury is going to need repair.'

'The eye is damaged too.' Lliam O'Hara was in deadly earnest now as he shook his head. 'I'm not at all sure we're going to be able to save it, but I won't know for sure until we get him under the anaesthetic. My God, what sort of people could do this?'

No one answered. They had seen it all before. It didn't make understanding any easier.

'Okay, let's get him into theatre. How about next of kin, Sister?'

'I'll talk to the police officer and see if we can contact anyone.'

'Would you like me to do it, Sister?' Gemma said. 'I gather the constable is waiting in reception.'

'If he's hoping for any kind of statement you can tell him to forget it,' John Sinclair said bluntly. 'There's no way this old chap will be talking to anyone for a while yet.'

'I'll tell him we'll let him know, sir.'

She went off in search of the police officer and found him standing anxiously in reception. 'Didn't they offer you a cup of tea?'

'Oh, sure.' He was young and good-looking. 'Couldn't really face it though. How's the patient?'

'Not too good I'm afraid.'

'No.' His mouth was set. 'All for three pounds. It makes you sick, doesn't it? He looked a right mess.'

Gemma could only nod. 'I wonder if you could let us have any details? Name, next of kin. We'll have to try and contact someone.'

There was precious little. A pension book, an address, no next of kin. Gemma finally went to lunch, ate in silence and returned to the unit. Niall Barratt had been right. She was beginning to wonder if she really did know what life was all about. But she was certainly finding out.

She was almost late next morning, rushing breathlessly into Sister's office and accepting a look of silent reproach as she drew up a chair and drew out her notebook for morning report. The familiar routine closed comfortingly in about her. Her responses became automatic.

'You'll be pleased to know that Mr West, the mugging victim, spent a fairly comfortable night,' Sister said. 'He is conscious but still badly shocked. Mr Sinclair will see him again today but any further surgery on the damaged eye is probably going to have to wait for a while until the patient's condition is generally more stable.'

'Have any relatives been located, Sister?'

'Unfortunately no. It rather looks as if there aren't any, but the police are continuing their inquiries. Obviously if none can be found we shall have to get Social Services and the various welfare organisations involved so that he isn't sent out of hospital to cope alone. Not that that is likely to be for some time yet.' She moved on. 'The road traffic accident cases. Paul Simms is still very poorly but making slight progress. The vital thing is to begin physiotherapy as soon as possible on the injured hip.'

The list was gone through and they all filed out of the office, the day's routine in full swing.

Coming back from coffee-break, Gemma was intercepted by Sister Pepper who happened to be coming out of the treatment room. 'Ah, Staff, I noticed from the list that you haven't taken your full quota of leave yet this year.'

'Yes, that's right, Sister.'

'Well you still have a week owing to you. Have you any particular dates you want to book? As the new-comer you're at the bottom of the list for choice this time, I'm afraid.'

'That's all right,' Gemma smiled quickly. 'I really don't mind. I've no special preferences.'

'Well don't leave it too long, anyway. You have to take your full quota before the end of the year so let me know fairly soon, will you?'

'Yes, of course, Sister.' The telephone rang and Jan Pepper returned to the office. So what am I going to do with a week's leave I don't really want? Gemma mused. She was in Recovery doing the routine checks on Mr West when Sister put her head round the door.

'Admission on its way, Staff. You'll be needed.'

Gemma signalled quietly to the second year nurse to take over and hurried after the retreating figure, already aware of the approaching ambulance sirens. Her gaze made a rapid but calm inspection of the instruments and the unit was suddenly full as the doors opened and the patient was lifted on to the examination couch. Gemma began assisting Sister Travers to remove the blood-stained clothing.

'We'd better get an immediate cross-match and start transfusions.' John Sinclair, mask pulled down, was working steadily, blocking her view of the man's face, but Gemma knew he was young.

'This arm is broken.'

By now the neurological registrar had arrived and was busily making his own rapid assessment of things. There were so many figures working quietly but quickly around the bed that Gemma scarcely noticed who they were.

'Keep checking his blood pressure, Staff.' John Sinclair moved aside, allowing her to apply the cuff to the patient's arm. It was the first chance she had actually had to see him properly and she became aware that her hands faltered, that she felt slightly sick. The fair hair was matted with blood. It might have been Bill lying there, except that reason told her he wasn't really anything like Bill. It was only that, for a few brief seconds, there had been some fleeting resemblance, imagination playing a cruel trick.

She was unaware that she had actually whispered Bill's name aloud or that she was staring, until a voice rapped sharply, 'I would suggest that unless you intend making yourself useful, you get out of the way, Nurse. This is hardly the time for day-dreaming.'

She came back to reality with a jerk, only to experience another, even greater shock as she found herself staring into the darkly sombre eyes which regarded her with such open hostility.

'Please God, don't let it be,' she mouthed silently. But as her gaze rose agonisingly to the taut face watching her, she knew that it was only too true.

Niall Barratt moved her sharply aside. 'If you're going to get squeamish, take yourself out and put your head between your knees. But don't you dare faint in here.'

The colour flew back to her cheeks. 'I have no intention of fainting, sir. I am perfectly all right.' Her mouth was clenched as she turned to John Sinclair. 'The blood pressure is falling, sir.' It was a relief that everyone was too involved to notice her flushed cheeks.

There was a tight feeling in the pit of her stomach as she steeled herself to working beside Niall Barratt, only to recognise the galling fact that, as far as he was concerned, she might have been a total stranger. More than once their hands met, sending a quiver of shock running through her as she bent to swab blood away in order to make the examination easier, but his reaction was one of cold indifference. She was still shaking when he straightened up, tugging the mask from his face and revealing lines of weariness.

'We'll get him straight into theatre. I've no choice. Both legs are going to have to come off. They're too badly crushed and he's lost a hell of a lot of blood.'

Gemma felt and shared the silent wave of shock and pity which enveloped them all, but there was no time to dwell on it.

'I'll scrub now. Rush the X-rays through, will you, Sister.' He turned to John Sinclair. 'I take it you'll be in on this one?'

The two men walked out together and Gemma applied herself vigorously to the task of cleaning up. Even if she had tried, she couldn't have explained to herself why she should suddenly feel so drained.

Laura Clarke was making a list of replacement surgical supplies which would be needed. 'Are you down for first or second lunch?'

'First I think, Sister.'

'In that case, when you've finished here you may as well go.'

Gemma paused and glanced toward the doors which led to theatre. 'Do you think he's going to make it?'

Sister shrugged. 'Your guess is as good as mine. He's in a pretty bad way and the shock of having both legs amputated has to be taken into account as well as the fact that he has fairly extensive head injuries as well. A great deal will depend on what happens when they take him off the life-support system temporarily to see whether he shows any sign of being able to breathe for himself. He's young, that much is on his side—and the fact that Mr Barratt is operating.'

Gemma's mouth felt dry and she had to swallow hard before she could speak. 'Yes, I suppose so. But . . . well, what exactly is he doing on this unit?'

'Mr Barratt?' Sister reached for a sterile suture pack. 'Surely you knew? Mr Barratt is in charge here. This is his own special baby, you might say. His dream child. He's certainly worked long enough for it.'

Gemma stared. 'But I thought he was a paediatric registrar.'

'Yes, indeed, so he is—or *was*, among other things. He also happens to be a general surgeon with a special interest in orthopaedic surgery. But of course, you've only recently joined us, haven't you, and Mr Barratt has been away attending a conference, so I suppose you don't actually know anything about his history or his family.'

Gemma felt her hand tighten involuntarily on the cold steel of the trolley. 'His family?'

'Yes indeed, a tragic business. His wife and son, you know.'

'I . . . I hadn't realised he was married.'

'Oh yes. She was a nurse, as a matter of fact. They had a son. They were both killed driving to meet him one day.' Sister shook her head. 'It was a head-on collision. A lorry driver had apparently fallen asleep at the wheel. Anyway, Mrs Barratt was killed instantly. The little boy died later. For a long time we all thought Mr Barratt would never get over it. It changed him terribly. Then suddenly he seemed to pick up the pieces and that's when he first began to fight for this unit. In a way I suppose you might say it kept him sane, gave him something to live for.' She sighed. 'The poor man certainly knows what tragedy is all about.'

Gemma knew the colour had drained from her face, leaving it ashen. Niall Barratt married. It seemed incredible that she had never even considered it, and a wave of shame hit her. All this time she had imagined she was the only one who had ever suffered . . .

She bent over her work, glad to hide the sudden tears. How could she have been such a complete and utter fool?

'You can go to lunch now, Staff.'

Gemma made some vague response and walked blindly from the room, just as the doors of the operating wing opened and Niall came out, dragging off his mask.

She stopped in her tracks but the words she wanted to say were stuck in her throat and he stared at her with a kind of icy contempt before striding away.

'Niall.' There was a look of blatant appeal in her eyes as she ran after him. 'Sir!'

His eyes were dark and unsmiling as he turned, frowning impatiently. 'Is it really important, Staff? I have to be back in theatre in ten minutes.'

It was like talking to a stranger, except that the face was the same, perhaps a little more weary. Suddenly Gemma found herself battling against an urge to rush into his arms, to say that now she understood. All these years she had been clinging to a ghost and he was right. She *had* been afraid of letting herself fall in love again in case she got hurt. But she knew now that the only thing that mattered was his love.

'I have to speak to you. To say . . . I'm sorry.'

'There's no need.' His voice cut her off abruptly. 'I'm sure I can take it that kind of incident won't happen again.'

He was already turning away and she felt her heart contract with misery as she followed him. 'I didn't mean that. I meant . . .' Suddenly she felt hurt and confused. 'Why?' She flung the word at him. 'Why didn't you tell me? At least give me a chance to understand.'

'I didn't see that any explanation was necessary.' His eyes narrowed as he looked at her. 'Or are you trying to say you wouldn't have accepted the job on the unit if you'd known I was in charge? But of course, that would be fairly typical, wouldn't it? Anything rather than face up to a challenge.' The contempt in his eyes was so clear that she flinched. It was only by a supreme effort that she managed to stand her ground.

'That wasn't what I meant.'

'No.' The cool gaze slid over her. 'Then I can't imagine why we're standing here wasting time.'

Her hand shot out, unthinkingly, to detain him when he would have walked away. 'Niall, please. I meant . . . Why didn't you tell me about your wife and child? I would have understood. I do understand, as I never did before.'

She felt the muscles of his arm tense beneath her fingers before he looked at her.

'I'm not in the habit of discussing my personal affairs with anyone, and I certainly don't intend to begin now. In any case, I don't see that my private life need concern you. You've made it pretty clear that you aren't interested.' He detached himself quietly from her grasp and she watched him walk away, a sudden, terrible coldness in her heart. It was too late. She had rejected her one chance and he would never forgive her for the hurt she had so unwittingly inflicted.

'Goodbye, Niall.' Her lips moved soundlessly. 'I love you.' But he didn't look back.

# CHAPTER FOURTEEN

SHE SLEPT badly again and woke next morning feeling heavy-eyed and lethargic. A fact which didn't go unnoticed by Sister.

'Are you all right, Staff?'

'Oh, yes thank you, Sister. Going in for a cold, I expect.'

'Yes, you're looking distinctly peaky.' The shrewd gaze assessed her. 'Have you given any more thought to the leave you still have owing?'

'No. Sorry, Sister, I'm afraid I haven't.'

'Well do, please. I like to keep my rota up to date and I disapprove of nurses not taking their full entitlement. Leave isn't a luxury, you know. It's a necessity, especially in a job like ours.'

'I'll bear it in mind, Sister, and I'll definitely let you know by the end of the week. Will that be all right?'

Gemma walked along the corridor towards Recovery, asking herself miserably what on earth she was going to do with herself for one whole week of enforced idleness. A glance in the mirror told her that perhaps it wouldn't be a bad thing, however much she hated the idea. Unhappiness was playing havoc with her looks, but somehow the prospect of seven days of nothing but her own company didn't seem an ideal solution.

She sighed heavily and went back to her work, wishing her heart wouldn't thud quite so painfully every time the swing doors opened and a white-coated figure came towards her.

This is ridiculous, she told herself. Sooner or later their paths were bound to cross, but the prospect of seeing Niall was something she thrust to the back of her mind. Hours of lying awake hadn't brought any answers. Perhaps because there weren't any, she thought desperately, as she made her way to Recovery to start the morning's routine checks. In fact the only thing she knew with any certainty was that working in close proximity to him was not only going to be unbearable from now on, it would be impossible.

She studied the face of the man in the bed and was recording the blood pressure reading when Sister came into the room.

'How's he doing?' Sister made her own observations, checking the drip and studying the chart she received from Gemma. 'I see he still hasn't recovered consciousness even temporarily.'

'No, Sister.'

'Mm. Well that isn't totally surprising, under the circumstances. What was the blood loss?'

'Almost five litres.'

'And what about the urine output?'

'That seems quite good. So is the cerebral veinous pressure. He's warm and his colour is good too.' Gemma straightened the covers over the bed cage. 'I suppose it isn't only the accident and the operation he has to survive. It's what comes afterwards, when he learns that he's lost both legs.'

'People manage to make extraordinary adjustments. It's one of the things you soon learn on this unit.' Sister smiled. 'The things you imagine are impossible aren't always. Miracles do sometimes still happen.'

Not to me, unfortunately, Gemma thought wanly as she tidied up and generally made the patient as comfortable as possible. She was pushing the bed curtains aside when the door opened and, thinking it was Sister returning, she turned with a smile to present the forgotten Kardex which lay on the locker. 'I was just about to bring it to the office, Sister . . .' Her voice faded. 'Niall.'

For a moment he didn't move as he looked at her. Just for a second she thought she saw a brief gleam of something—surprise, pleasure—as the challenging eyes met hers. Then it was gone and his voice was tight with politeness.

'I'd like to make a quick examination of the patient, Staff Nurse, please.'

It was like a slap in the face and her cheeks were flushed as she said, 'Yes, sir,' and stood aside as he brushed past her. The curtains made a convenient natural barrier between them and she was glad of it as a wave of faintness hit her. He was like a cold, distant stranger.

John Sinclair smiled in her direction as he came into the room and she flickered a response, averting her eyes from the dark hair curling over the collar of Niall Barratt's coat as he bent to make his examination.

'He's been unconscious for twenty-four hours. I'm not too worried at this stage, but I don't want it to go on too long, obviously.' He straightened up. 'Ophthalmoscope please, Staff.'

Gemma moved quickly, biting her lip as her fingers made contact with his.

'I'd say we can leave him till tomorrow morning, then try stopping the ventilator just for a few seconds to see what happens.'

'That's pretty much what I thought. We'll stop the drugs too, so that we get a better idea of his true condition.'

Gemma was adjusting the over-bed light when Sister returned in search of the missing Kardex. Her expression became immediately harassed.

'Oh, good morning, Mr Barratt. I hadn't realised you wanted to make an examination.'

'That's quite all right, Sister. I just decided to pop in on my way to theatre to see how he's doing. I'm going to listen to his heart if Staff Nurse will be good enough to loosen his clothing.'

Gemma jumped, cheeks reddening, only to see Sister's hand raised in her direction. 'That's all right, Mr Barratt. I'll take over from Staff Nurse so that she can get on with her other duties, if you have no objection?'

Gemma felt herself come under a brief but cool scrutiny before he shook his head.

'Not at all, Sister.'

She fled, clutching the card in a shaking hand without a single glance in his direction. Outside she paused to gasp for breath and to face the fact that working with him was going to be every bit as impossible as she had imagined.

She took a couple of aspirins with her lunch, skipped the shepherd's pie and was on her way back to the unit when Dick Foster caught up with her.

'Dick. Should you be here?'

He scanned the length of the corridor. 'Probably not, but as long as no one sees . . .' He held her arm. 'Look, I have to talk to you—to someone—or I'll go mad. Please.'

She tore her glance away from the clock. 'I take it it's about Sue?'

'How did you guess?' He said it humourlessly and she saw the nervous gesture as he pushed the hair from his eyes. 'We can't go on like this. I'm cracking up. My work is suffering. Sooner or later at this rate I'm going to lose my job.'

'Oh no. Surely things can't be that bad?' Gemma was appalled.

'Can't they? I can't sleep. I can't eat. They're not exactly the best qualifications for my kind of work. The patients tend to notice if a doctor nods off in mid-sentence.'

Her hand tightened sympathetically over his. 'Oh, Dick, I had no idea!'

He stared at it, then at her, and laughed again. 'I suppose you haven't heard the latest, either. They say I'm actually carrying on with another woman. Can you imagine it? How long do you think it will be before Sue hears it and believes it, the way things are at the moment?'

Gemma fought down a feeling of panic as she remembered Sue's words. 'But that's crazy. I don't believe it!'

He looked at her, pityingly. 'My dear Gemma, you obviously don't know the full irony of it. *You* are supposed to be the other woman.'

'What?' She felt the colour drain from her face as she stared at him. 'You can't be serious?'

His mouth twisted grimly. 'You know what the grape-vine is. If there isn't a scandal, invent one.'

'But they can't!'

'My love, they already have. I wouldn't have known except that someone asked me if it was true. It's smouldering. Give it time and it will break out into a forest fire. Which is why I've got to try and get things straightened out with Sue, to make her understand. You do see that, don't you?'

Gemma wondered whether she was capable of understanding anything any more. She and Dick? Her eyes closed in a brief but horrific image of Sue hearing the story and knew it must never happen.

The door at the end of the corridor opened and she said quickly, 'Look, I'll have to go. I should have been on duty thirty seconds ago.'

'So should I. How about tonight? Can we meet, talk properly? Somewhere where we won't be over-heard.'

'I'm off at six-thirty.'

'Fine. I'll meet you just round the corner.'

'But I may be late.'

'That's all right, I'll wait.'

He disappeared along the corridor, leaving Gemma standing rooted to the spot, a hundred different thoughts rushing through her brain and none of them very palatable. She saw, vaguely, the small group of figures coming towards her. Niall Barratt barely glanced in her direction but she sensed his disapproval. It was enough to tell her that he had seen her with Dick, and she didn't doubt that he had drawn his own inevitable conclusions.

It was after seven by the time she finally ran down the drive and got into the waiting car. 'Sorry I'm late. I just couldn't get away. Everything went wrong.'

'That's okay.' Dick manoeuvred the car into the traffic, his face tense. 'I thought we could go to a small place I know not far from here.' He glanced quickly at her. 'Sue and I used to go there quite a lot at one time, before things got complicated. The food is good and reasonable. Are you hungry?'

'I'm not sure.' She hadn't thought about it, or anything, except in a dazed sort of way which didn't bring any solutions. She stared out of the window. It was starting to rain. 'It's all a bit of a nightmare isn't it? So ludicrous.'

His hand came over hers. 'Don't worry about it. We'll sort something out.'

The irony of it was, she thought, that there was nothing to sort out. No happy ever after. She sighed, thinking of Sue, and knew she was being selfish—perhaps even a little jealous? The idea was too uncomfortable and she was glad when they drew up at the restaurant. It looked small and unpretentious but inside a pleasant warmth met them and the surroundings, she noticed, as they were led to a table, were fresh and attractive. It was almost a pity that she wasn't in any mood to appreciate them.

'What about something to eat?'

'Not particularly.' She forced a smile, feeling her stomach revolt at the thought of food, then realised he probably hadn't eaten a square meal for weeks. 'Actually something fairly light might be a good idea. I'm feeling a bit light-headed.'

'How about omelettes or seafood pancakes? I do know they're good.'

'Lovely.'

She sat looking round as he gave the order, but when the food came, tempting as it looked, she found herself toying with it.

'It wasn't such a good idea after all, was it?' Dick stared at their plates and pushed his aside. 'It's no good. Unless I get things straight with Sue, I'm not going to be able to go on like this.' He drained his glass of wine and looked at her. 'I've even been thinking along the lines of giving up my job and moving away. It's got that bad.'

She knew how he felt. 'Have you actually tried talking?'

He laughed mirthlessly. 'In passing, so to speak. Even on the rare occasions I've seen her, she hasn't seemed to want to talk.'

'It's possible that she doesn't know what to say because she can't see any answers.'

'She hasn't been at the flat in over a week.'

'No.' Gemma stirred her coffee, took a deep breath and said quietly, 'She's been staying at my flat.' She saw the look of disbelief on his face. 'I wanted to tell you. I've been begging her to see you and sort things out.'

'But then . . . Why? In God's name! It's crazy. I love her. I used to think she loved me.'

She reached for her own glass, not looking up as other people came into the restaurant. 'Dick, did you know she is pregnant?'

His mouth opened. 'Pre . . . ? Oh my God. But that's bloody marvellous!' He stopped and frowned. 'So why does she refuse to come home, at least to talk? For heaven's sake, we have to talk.'

'I don't think she can see that it will help. In fact, as far as Sue sees it, the baby is going to complicate things even more. I gather you won't be able to keep the flat. She'll have to give up her job fairly soon.' Her hand reached out. 'Dick, I can understand why she is worried.'

'But we can find some answer. People do.'

'*I* know that; so do you. But just at the moment Sue isn't thinking rationally.' She looked at his white face. 'She knows about the rumours too.'

'Oh my . . .'

'Not that I'm supposed to be involved,' she added quickly. 'I told her it was rubbish. I didn't realise then . . .'

Dick squeezed her hand. 'I'm more sorry than I can say that you've been dragged into this. I'll never forget it. I don't even know how to thank you.'

She smiled bleakly. 'Don't try. Just make sure the pair of you come to your senses. I don't know the answer, but I do have a kind of faith that things usually have a way of working themselves out.' She delved into her pocket and handed him her keys. 'Look, why not go over to my place now? It's Sue's night off. I'm sure all she really needs is the chance to see you alone, to talk. Don't be put off.'

He took the keys, looked at her, then leaned over the table and kissed her. 'Bless you. Some day I will make it up to you. But what about you?'

'Oh I'll be all right. I'll go and visit the nurses' home and beg cups of coffee from friends. You can always phone me later.'

'If you're sure.'

She nodded and they both got to their feet. 'You'd better get going. I'll come out to the car with you. It won't take me long to walk back to the hospital.'

They walked out to the car park. 'I really am grateful, Gemma.'

'Just sort it out.' She smiled, accepting his kiss, then watched as he drove away. For some minutes she stood in the rain, letting its coolness ease her headache. Then, with a sigh, she pulled up the collar of her coat and began to walk. One problem at least looked like being solved. If only she could put her own life back together so easily.

At first she paid no attention to the figure striding up beside her until a hand caught her in a vice-like grip and she found herself whirled round to face the angry features of Niall Barratt. For a few seconds shock made her feel faint; then relief took over and she said, indignantly, 'Oh, it's you. You frightened the life out of me, creeping up on me like that.'

'As it happens, I didn't creep.' In the half-light

from the street lamps she saw his mouth twist sardonically. 'I witnessed that touching little scene back in the restaurant there and followed you out. But of course, you were so wrapped up in each other and your cheap little . . . *assignation* that you didn't even notice.'

She heard herself gasp and tried to pull away. 'That isn't true.'

'Oh come on! I saw it with my own eyes.'

She swallowed hard, willing herself to stop trembling, but the shock of his nearness, his accusations, seemed to rob her of every shred of control. 'You don't understand.'

He laughed bitterly. 'Oh, I think I do, Gemma. I think I understand you very well. You don't want to get involved so you think married men are safer. That way you don't get hurt.'

This time she struggled furiously to get free of his grasp, feeling the tears sting at her lashes, but he merely tightened his grip on her arms.

'You do know that Dick Foster is married? But of course you do,' his voice sneered. 'I should have realised when I saw you together before. But then, I was crazy enough to care, to believe it couldn't be true.'

'You don't know what you're saying. It isn't like that at all! If only you'd give me a chance to explain.'

He shook her, drawing her closer. 'You crazy little fool! What you do with your life doesn't concern me. I've heard it all before, remember, and nothing has changed. You're still a coward, still running away.'

'No.' Her voice shook.

'Oh yes.' Suddenly his mouth came down on hers cruelly, hurting her with its savagery. For a second she tried to resist, her hands pressed against his chest as she struggled. Her body quivered with angry resentment. She didn't want his kisses, not like this. It was easy to say, but her body was playing the traitor. The more she fought the more insistent he became and suddenly she knew that she could never win. She loved him. Even if it meant being hurt all over again. With a moan she let her resistance fall away as her hands moved to the back of his neck, drawing him closer.

The sensuous mouth was dragging responses from her and she wanted it to go on for ever. His lips freed her for an instant and she murmured huskily, 'I love you,' feeling the warmth of his breath on her face. Then suddenly, with a violence which brought her crashing back to reality, he pushed her away, his eyes lashing her with contempt.

'You see. I was right. Nothing has changed.'

She could only stare at him, appalled, not understanding, shaking with humiliation.

'No. No, I love you.' Her voice was little more than a whisper and he laughed.

'I'm afraid I'm not prepared to take the risk, not a second time. You're not the only one who doesn't intend getting hurt. I've no intention of playing games, Gemma.'

Her mouth opened to deny it but he was already walking away and she stood trembling, feeling the tears coursing down her cheeks as she whispered, 'I love you,' knowing that even if he heard, he wouldn't care.

# CHAPTER FIFTEEN

MAKE-UP had done nothing to hide the pallor of her face. She still looked pale and drawn as she stood in the office next morning.

By the time she had got back to the flat it had been late. There had been a note from Dick saying simply, *Thanks for everything. We're going home. Will catch up with you later*. She had read it and felt too numb to care. All she wanted was to fall into bed to find a few hours of blissful oblivion, except that she hadn't been able to sleep as her brain had magnified the events of the evening, filling her with an even greater sense of misery and shame. The full irony of it had hit her round about dawn as she stood watching the first grey shafts of light appear. She had been afraid to fall in love because love only brought pain. Like a fool she had told herself it wasn't true and she had let it happen. She hugged her arms about her body in a self-protective embrace. But it *did* hurt. Far more than she could bear.

She had gone into the hospital early, her mind made up. 'If it won't cause too much inconvenience, Sister, I'd like to take my leave next week if possible. I know it's very short notice.'

Sister reached for the list. 'As it happens, it suits me ideally. Fixed something nice, have you?' Her eyes briefly studied the shadowed face but she kept her thoughts to herself.

'I thought I'd go and see my parents in Cornwall. They have a small farm not too far from the sea. I should be able to get plenty of exercise.'

'Good.' Sister smiled approvingly and Gemma made her way towards the unit. A week would give her time to think, to make plans. There was no future for her here. At least somewhere else she might eventually manage to pick up the pieces, and even if she couldn't forget, time might make the whole thing seem more bearable.

She didn't even think about Sue, so that it came as a surprise three days later as she was on her way to coffee to find herself waylaid by a figure so obviously elated and happy that it bubbled from her like a bottle of champagne. She hugged Gemma in the middle of the corridor, drawing some disapproving looks from a passing registrar.

'I had to catch you. I've been dying to tell you the news.'

They sat together in the cafeteria drinking coffee, Gemma listening, forcing herself to smile even though her mouth, the whole of her body, felt frozen.

'Everything's going to be all right!' Sue attacked a packet of biscuits with a satisfaction Gemma envied. 'I'll never be able to thank you enough.'

'I didn't do anything really.'

'Oh, but you did. You were right. Dick and I needed to talk. Somehow I'd got things all out of perspective.' She glanced at Gemma. 'Even those ridiculous rumours about Dick. I know there was nothing in them.'

'I told you there couldn't be. He loves you far too much.'

'Yes, I know. I'm lucky. Not only with Dick but everything else too.' She sighed happily. 'It's as if a huge cloud has been lifted and a miracle really has happened. Dick went and had a long talk with his boss.'

'You mean Niall Barratt?'

'Mm. Honestly, I've always thought the man was dishy but he's more than that. He's actually offered Dick a job on his team. Just imagine. More security, more pay—I can hardly believe it!'

Gemma had to battle with the sudden feeling of tightness in her throat. 'I'm so pleased for you. It's marvellous.'

'Yes, isn't it? Of course, we still won't be able to afford a house straight away, but we can get a bigger flat, one with a garden. Mr Barratt has even given us the address of a friend of his who is in the property business. And we'll be able to save for something bigger, gradually. Oh, Gemma, it's all a bit like a dream!'

Or a nightmare. It only proved all the more how much of an enigma the man was. The rest of the week passed in a state of tension in case she should see him, so that by Friday evening when she finally got into the car, suitcase neatly stowed in the boot, she wondered whether a week was going to be enough to bring her mind into any kind of state where she could make rational decisions.

Her parents greeted her arrival with their customary, gratifying reactions. Her father eyed her in his usual shrewd but silent way before he kissed her warmly and said, 'You should come more often. It's nice to see you home. Here, let me take that case up to your room.'

Gemma relinquished it and her mother kissed her, exclaiming disapprovingly that she was too thin and horribly pale.

'What on earth do they do to you at that place?'

She tutted and fussed and produced a huge supper. 'We'll soon put some fat on those bones. Can't you stay more than a week?'

Replete after the huge meal, Gemma settled in front of the fire, tired but dreading going up to her room to face hours of wakefulness. 'Sorry. I only wish I could.'

'Are they working you too hard, dear? You're looking very tired.'

She responded with a tight-lipped smile to her father's gentle query. 'No, I don't think so, Dad. Oh, it is hard work. But I love it. It's what I always wanted, you know that.'

'Well, couldn't you move a little nearer home?' her mother asked bluntly, knitting needles clicking. 'We don't see much of you, especially since Bill . . .' She broke off, a worried expression marring her still attractive features. 'We do worry about you, you know.'

'Yes, of course I do.' Gemma struggled to keep her voice even. 'To tell you the truth, I have been thinking lately that I could do with a bit of a change.'

'Everything's all right, is it?'

'Yes. Oh yes.' She felt herself flush beneath John Lawson's gaze and got up quickly to pour more coffee. 'It's only a thought. At least I've got a week to go over it in my mind.'

'Yes, well take it easy while you're here. Have a proper rest.'

For the first few days she did just that. The ridiculous thing was that it took so long even to begin to unwind.

I shall be back at Vincent's at this rate and still no plans made, Gemma thought as she strolled along the deserted beach, kicking at pebbles, picking up shells. It was a time of year she loved, when all the visitors had gone home.

The wind was chilly so she had wrapped up warmly in jeans and a thick sweater, but there was something about the breeze blowing through her hair after so many months of wearing it neatly tucked beneath a cap. She stood staring at the sea, its cold, pewter-grey waves crashing on to the darkened sand and receding gently. She loved the sea in all its moods, but today there was something depressing about it and she turned, sticking her hands into her pockets as she walked towards the outcrop of rocks at the far end of the stretch of sand. It was empty except for one other figure in the far distance. Not many people ventured out in winter, which was a pity she thought, because they missed the wilder kind of beauty.

Seagulls and wading birds paddled and soared noisily on the changing waterline, searching for food. It was all a matter of survival. And they seem far better at it than I am, the thought carried with her.

The wind stung her cheeks, drying the tears which had brought nothing more than temporary relief and left her with a headache, but at least she had come to some kind of decision. When she got back to the house she would write a letter of resignation and start looking for a job somewhere else, perhaps even abroad.

Her gaze went to scan the horizon. The distant figure was closer, striding purposefully along the cliff path. She could pick out the black of a sweater now and felt an unreasoned pang of irritation as he turned on to the narrow path which led to 'her' beach, invading her privacy.

She deliberately turned her back on him and

began to walk decisively in the opposite direction.
There would be a lot of things she would miss. Her
parents, friends. She realised she wouldn't even see
Sue and Dick's baby. It would be a huge break,
wrenching herself from everything she knew and
loved. For a crazy moment she toyed with the idea
of staying on and knew it was impossible. Niall was
right, she was too much of a coward to want to go
on seeing him, loving him and knowing it could
never be returned.

Gemma heard the sound of footsteps crunching
over the shingle behind her and wondered resentfully why, of all stretches of beach, the intruder had
to pick this one. She sighed. Another five minutes
and she would have to go back. She felt cold but it
wasn't a purely physical thing. For a moment she
stood with a hand pressed over her eyes, willing the
unhappiness to go away.

She looked up only slowly as the voice spoke
her name. At first she thought she had imagined it, until it came again. Then she turned to
stare disbelievingly at the figure coming towards
her.

'Niall?' Every fibre of her being told her that it
was her imagination playing tricks. Even if it were
true, why was he here? What more could he want?
Hadn't she suffered enough humiliation? She
stepped back, turning away.

'Gemma, wait.'

She froze and looked back. He looked older, his
face was etched with faint lines of exhaustion and
there was a tension about his jaw as he came closer.
'I have to talk to you. Please.' Then, incredibly, she
was in his arms. It was still like a dream, except that
he was warm, strong, all male.

Tears blurred her eyes, blinding her to the look

of anguish on his face. Her entire being screamed, '*Caution*', and she shook her head wordlessly, willing him to go away, unaware that she had actually whispered it aloud. She was just beginning to get her emotions under control. It wasn't fair that he should stir them up again, fling more accusations at her.

'Gemma, please. I know I deserve it, but I had to come.'

'How did you find me?' Her voice shook with cold fury.

'It was easy. The hospital have your home address on record. I spoke to your parents.'

Her face whitened. 'You did what?'

'You didn't tell them.' He looked at her deeply, searchingly, and she felt her heart thudding so fast that she was afraid she was going to faint.

'What was there to say?'

He moved closer, his grip on her arms tightening. 'You could have told them that I behaved like a fool.' His mouth was very close. She wanted to move away but couldn't. 'You could have said that I hurt you unforgivably, simply because I didn't understand.'

She stared at him. 'What are you trying to say?'

'That I know now what happened, and I must have been crazy to believe otherwise. Will you ever be able to forgive me?'

Her every instinct yearned to say yes. To forget and let him wipe out the memories with one kiss, but she pulled away.

'It's too late.'

She saw his face darken. His grip relaxed and she turned away quickly before he could see the tears in her eyes. 'I'm going away.'

'No.' He made some stifled sound, then forced

her to turn and look at him again. 'You can't. I won't let you run away again.'

'I have to. Don't you see that?'

'No, I don't.' He groaned and drew her into his arms, keeping her there, kissing her until she wanted to beg him to stop. 'I've admitted I was a fool. I can't let you go.'

'But don't you see, you were right!' Tears were coursing down her cheeks now. 'I *am* afraid of being hurt. I don't know that I wouldn't fail you.'

'Oh my darling, crazy little . . . Don't you know there's no way you could ever fail me because I won't let you be afraid, ever again.' He kissed her lips, then the tears. 'I know you were hurt once, but we have each other now and the future. I need you.' His voice rasped. 'I love you. I want to spend the rest of my life with you.'

There was only a second's hesitation before she went into his arms, her head against his chest, until he tilted her face up to kiss her again.

'You once said you loved me. I tried not to listen. Now I want to hear you say it.'

'I love you,' she said simply. 'I always have. I always will. For the rest of my life.'

He cupped her face in his hands. 'For once I can't argue with that powerful sense of dedication, my darling.'

'But I thought you said it was dangerous?'

'Ah.' He smiled down at her. 'But only if it is misguided—and I don't think there's any danger of that, do you?'

She smiled and kissed him again. 'None at all.' The wind carried all the ghosts away. There was only now, and this man she loved, and their future together.

# Give the Rose of Romance on Mother's Day.

**DESIRABLE PROPERTY**
Catherine George

**A SUMMER IDYLL**
Betty Neels

**THE ONLY ONE**
Penny Jordan

**NEVER IN A LIFETIME**
Lilian Peake

Bring someone some romance this Mother's Day. Four brand new titles from Mills and Boon, attractively gift wrapped for £4.40.

Look for this gift pack where you buy Mills and Boon romances – it's available from 8th February 1985.

# The Rose of Romance

# Doctor Nurse Romances

Amongst the intense emotional pressures of modern medical life, doctors and nurses often find romance. Read about their lives and loves in the other three Doctor Nurse titles available this month.

### NO DOCTORS, PLEASE
*by Lydia Balmain*

"I don't want a *good* husband, I want a rich, exciting one." And with that in mind, Jenny Speed, whirlwind Staff Nurse of the Royal's private ward, has sworn never to go out with a member of the medical staff. By coincidence, so has gorgeous orthopaedic consultant, Gerard Sterne…

### THORN-TREE MIDWIFE
*by Barbara Perkins*

When Staff Nurse Kate Raven takes a post as a midwife in Central Africa, she imagines that she has left her family troubles behind her. So she is not best pleased to find that handsome Dr Nicholas Kyle of Mutala Hospital is a cousin by marriage…

### HEART OF A SURGEON
*by Alexina Rawdon*

Theatre Sister Alison Wood is determined to get a job in Parkleigh Hospital's new cardiology unit. But Alison's hopes are dashed when she meets the head of the team — for Greg Verney is not only a brilliant heart surgeon, but he's also the man who jilted her two years ago!

## Mills & Boon
## the rose of romance